Jelly

Jo Cotterill

 YELLOW JACKET

This is a work of fiction. Any references to historical events, real people, or real places are used fictitiously. Other names, characters, places, and events are products of the author's imagination, and any resemblance to actual events or places or persons, living or dead, is entirely coincidental.

YELLOW JACKET
an imprint of Little Bee Books

251 Park Avenue South, New York, NY 10010
Text copyright © 2018 by Jo Cotterill
All rights reserved, including the right of
reproduction in whole or in part in any form.
Originally published in the UK by Piccadilly Press,
an imprint of Bonnier Zaffre Ltd, in 2018
Yellow Jacket and associated colophon
are trademarks of Little Bee Books.
Manufactured in the United States of America LAK 1219
First U.S. Edition

10 9 8 7 6 5 4 3 2 1

Library of Congress Cataloging-in-Publication
Data is available upon request.
ISBN 978-1-4998-1006-6
yellowjacketreads.com

For information about special discounts on bulk purchases,
please contact Little Bee Books at sales@littlebeebooks.com.

Chapter 1

"Do it now, Jelly! Please!"

"All right," I say, "but check the door for Mr. Lenck."

My friend Kayma scuttles to the open classroom door and sticks her head out into the corridor. "No sign," she says. "Quick!"

I take a deep breath and pull myself up very straight. My friends start to giggle because they know what's coming next, and a ripple of interest spreads across the rest of the class. People turn midconversation, and their eyes light up when they see me standing by my chair. Everyone knows what I can do.

I walk very carefully and precisely over to the teacher's desk at the front of the room, turning in my toes. Then I whip round, look out over the classroom, and sniff slightly. There's another burst of giggling. I snap my head to the right and say, making my voice as nasal as possible, "Marshall, I don't know *what* you think you're doing."

The class, including Marshall, shrieks with laughter.

"It's your own time you're wasting," I add, frowning sternly at him.

More laughter. Marshall guffaws so hard he bends forward over his table.

I roll my eyes to the ceiling, with its square panels and long rectangular lights, and say, "Sometimes I don't know *why* I bother."

The giggles are suddenly silenced, and I know what *that* means.

A nasal voice behind me says, "Angelica Waters, I don't know *what* you think you're doing." The voice belongs to Mr. Lenck, our teacher, and its tone and inflections are almost exactly the same as my impression.

I turn to smile widely at him. "Oh, hello, Mr. Lenck. Did you have a nice lunch?"

Mr. Lenck rolls his eyes to the ceiling, just as I did a

moment earlier, sighs and says, "It's in one ear and out the other with you, Angelica, isn't it?"

"Sorry, Mr. Lenck," I say. "It's a compliment really."

"Doing impressions of your teachers is a *compliment*?" Mr. Lenck repeats, raising his eyebrows.

"You're so expressive," I explain. "And you have really good catchphrases."

One corner of Mr. Lenck's mouth twitches. Teachers can never stay cross with me for long. It's not exactly *rude* what I do. It's funny. Even Mr. Lenck finds it hard not to laugh when I do Mr. Harding, the janitor. "Sit down," is all he says now.

He starts taking attendance, and I sit back down next to my two best friends, Kayma and Sanvi. Kayma, her long braids swinging forward into her face, gives me the thumbs-up. Sanvi smiles at me, but in a sort of half-admiring, half-appalled kind of way. She has big brown eyes that go very wide when I do something risky. Out of the three of us, Sanvi is the goody-goody. Her family's pretty strict, so she always does what she's told.

Once attendance is over, we go into the hall for assembly. I prepare to be bored, but Mrs. Belize, the principal, has an announcement. "As most of you know, we always have a talent show at the end of the semester." She pauses dramatically and then says, with jazz hands: "The K Factor!"

A murmur of excitement goes through the kids squashed cross-legged on the floor. K stands for Kingswood, the name of our school. Anyone can enter, and if you win, you get your name on The K Factor trophy, which stands in the cabinet by the school office.

I've entered every single year but never won it. Last year I did a comedy sketch with Kayma and Sanvi and we came in third. But I've been getting better and better at impressions, and everyone loves them. This could be my year.

Mrs. Belize goes on: "This morning's assembly is about famous performers and the things they've done. And the added bonus is . . . they're all children!"

The projection screen rolls down, and she starts showing us videos of kids from around the world doing amazing things, like playing the piano with their feet, or doing twenty backflips in a row, or building a tower of forty-three Life Savers. "Now," says Mrs. Belize as the presentation ends, "I'm not saying we've got the next Mozart at Kingswood. Or the next Harry Potter. Yes, Angelica?"

My hand has shot up. "Mrs. Belize," I say kindly, "you do know Harry Potter isn't real, right?"

The whole school laughs, and my heart thrills at the sound.

"Not real?" Mrs. Belize pretends to be shocked. Then her voice changes tone. "Thank you, Angelica. I leave it to you to point that out. I was meaning, of course, that maybe some of you can do magic tricks, or perhaps—*yes*, Angelica?"

"Is flying on a broom allowed in school?" I ask politely.

"If you're able to pull that off, Angelica, we'll all be very impressed," says Mrs. Belize dryly. "Now, the auditions aren't for several weeks, but I know some of you like lots of time to plan your acts, maybe writing scripts, rehearsing, or finding time outside of school to practice with your friends. And as usual, we'll have a special guest judge for the finals!"

She makes this sound very exciting, but we all know that the special guest judge is usually her daughter Julie, who once had a part in *Glee*. We're not supposed to talk as we file out of the hall, but of course everyone is whispering to one another.

"You *so* have to do your impressions," Kayma hisses at

me. "Mr. Harding, for one. And Mr. Lenck."

Sanvi whispers from behind, "Is that really a good idea? I mean, don't you think people will be upset if Jelly does impressions of them?"

"Course not." Kayma waves away this suggestion. "And if they do, who cares? We're leaving at the end of the year!"

Sanvi lapses into appalled silence.

"Thing is," Kayma says in a normal tone as we head down the hall, "what are *we* going to do? Me and Sanvi?"

"We can't do comedy sketches without Jelly," Sanvi breaks in. "We're not funny enough."

"Speak for yourself," Kayma retorts. "I'm *hilarious*."

I laugh. "I'll help you figure out what to do. There's loads of time."

"Maybe I could be a magician sawing Sanvi in half," Kayma mutters as we enter the classroom.

As we settle into afternoon classes, I am buzzing inside. I love performing. And here's my chance to do the thing I'm best at—the thing everyone loves about me—onstage, in front of an audience! I can't *wait*.

Chapter 2

"Hey, Jelly! Wait up!" Will Matsunaga catches up with me in the playground after school. He has cropped ginger hair and freckles that multiply if he so much as looks at sunlight. "I hear you're going to do impressions in The K Factor. I've got a suggestion for you." He glances sideways at two friends who've followed along behind.

"What is it?" I ask.

"A walrus," he says, and his friends start to snicker.

"A walrus?" I repeat. A chill races through my veins, and my hands tremble slightly. Walruses are big and fat. I look down at myself, wider around the waist than any of the other girls in class.

Will and his friends are now openly laughing—and waiting to see what I'll do.

The thing is, when people say hurtful things to you, you have a choice about how you respond. Option One is the most obvious: Tell them what they said was hurtful and ask them to apologize.

I never take Option One. Option Two: Laugh it off.

I stick my two index fingers in the corners of mouth, like tusks, blow out my cheeks, and pull my shoulders up to the sides of my head, hiding my neck. Then I let out a kind of loud, low growl.

Will's face lights up in delight. "Hey, that's really good! You totally look like one! Put that in your act!" He and his friends run off, laughing—but now they're laughing *with* me, not *at* me.

That's why I always take Option Two.

I set off for home. Mom started letting me go on my own this year, now that I'm eleven. The route takes me across three main roads, down a short alley between houses, and along one side of a park. I slow down when I get to the park. Most people do, I notice. When they walk along gray pavements spotted with ancient gum, they hurry, anxious to move along. When they reach a path bordered by grass and flower beds, they slow down.

If you want to do impressions, you have to be good at observation. I like watching people, they're all good material.

I speed up the rest of the way, turning left at the end of the park and into the cul-de-sac that leads to our block of apartments, low and squat and ugly. We live on the first floor, so there's no garden. I let myself in the main entrance door and run up the stairs, taking them two at a time. Our door is white and could do with a repaint, like most of the apartments in this building. I use the other key on my key ring to open it and call, "Hi!" to my mom. She's working in her bedroom at a tiny desk. She runs a beauty products business, selling mascara and eye shadow to people. It means there's a LOT of makeup in our apartment.

"Hey!" she calls back. "You OK? I'm just finishing up an order, and then I'll come out for a cup of tea."

"No worries!"

My bedroom is cozy, by which I mean small, but I don't mind because it's big enough for me (even though I am not small, as anyone would tell you). The wallpaper is flowery but not in an in-your-face way. It's peeling off a bit in one corner which Mom says is because of moisture, so we put my chest of drawers there to hide it. I drop my schoolbag on the floor, kick off my shoes, and jump onto my bed.

I like school. I like my friends and I like making people laugh, but somehow I always feel tired at the end of the day.

I lie on the bed and stare at the ceiling. It's been a really good day, I tell myself. My impression of Mr. Lenck that made the whole class laugh, the announcement of The K Factor . . . Kayma and Sanvi being cool as ever.

But . . . but . . .

Walrus. I hear it over and over again, that taunt, and even though it was just one small moment in an otherwise good day, it feels like it's spoiled everything. It hurt. It always hurts. And no matter how much I tell myself it doesn't matter, that it doesn't bother me . . . it does. It bothers me a lot.

I reach beneath the pillow under my head, because there's something I do at times like this: when it feels like I'm two people, and the other Jelly, the other me, is screaming in frustration.

Under the pillow is my special book. It has a pink cover with shell patterns on it and it says, "I'M A PART-TIME MERMAID" on the front. Mom bought it for me last Christmas. It's very girly, and exactly the sort of thing people assume I'll like. It's useful camouflage because the cover suggests I'll be drawing pictures of hearts and unicorns inside, so Mom never bothers to look through it. If she did, she'd get a shock.

I find a blank page and reach for my (matching, shiny pink) pen. Then I write:

Walrus

A large flippered mammal
loud, lively
lolloping around
Comical in its thick skin
Blubber pierced
By spiky splinters of insults
From slim seals in
            school uniform

I hear the floor in Mom's room creak and I just have time to shove the book under my pillow before she appears in the doorway. "Hey," she says, smiling. "How's it going?"

I smile back cheerfully. "Good!"

Chapter 3

Mom drinks green tea, which smells funny but she says it's good for you. I like normal tea, strong and with a spoonful of sugar. I do an impression of Mrs. Belize telling us about The K Factor, and she laughs. "You've got her to a T."

"I'm going to do impressions this year," I say.

"On your own? That's brave. Ooh!" She suddenly springs up. "I got you a doughnut! Hang on . . ." I hear the bread box clang in the kitchen and then she reappears, holding a paper bag. "Here you go."

"Yum! Jelly and sugar, my favorite. Thanks, Mom."

She sits back down, smiling at me. My mom is very beautiful. Her face is a slim oval shape, and her eyes are green, like mine. When she smiles they crinkle at the corners, and you can see the layers of foundation and powder crinkle too. Her eyelashes are always coated in mascara, making them look long and fluttery, and she uses heavy black eyeliner on her top and bottom lids, even during the daytime. Her hair is light brown really, but she dyes it white-blonde. She's slim as anything because she does yoga every morning. When she walks down the street, people turn to look at her because she's so striking. I feel proud when I'm with her.

I bite into my doughnut and jelly oozes down my chin. Mom laughs and reaches out with one perfectly nail-painted finger to wipe it away. "I read once it's impossible to eat a doughnut without licking your lips."

"Challenge accepted!" I say.

She sighs a little. "I miss doughnuts."

"You could have one," I say. "One wouldn't matter."

"It's not worth it," she replies, shaking her head. "You make the most of it while you're still young!" She takes a sip of her tea. "I'm going out tonight, OK?"

Oh. Suddenly the doughnut sticks in my throat.

I cough and take a gulp of tea. "With Chris?" I say, not looking at her.

"Yes," she says.

Chris is her boyfriend. I don't like him much. I don't know why Mom does. He's . . . well, he's just not all that nice. Mom won't hear a word against him, which is strange because sometimes when they've been out together she comes home quite upset. He says stuff that isn't very kind, but she says he doesn't mean it really.

I think he *does* mean it, and I hate it when he spends time here. I suppose I'm glad that at least they're going out tonight so he won't be *here*. "Is Rosie coming over?" I ask. Rosie is fourteen. She lives upstairs and is totally obsessed with her phone.

"Yes, she'll be here at seven."

"OK," I say. I look down at the table and don't say anything else.

"What's the matter?" asks Mom.

"Nothing," I say, and I smile at her. "I'm fine."

She finishes her tea and gets up. "I've got to get back to work. Three new orders came in half an hour ago! The new eye shadow range is just zipping off the shelves. I'm buying in bulk, but I think I'll have to up my orders . . .

and I need to get back to this girl Maisie who wants to sign up as an agent. . . ." She drifts off, calling, "Shout if you need anything!"

I finish my doughnut and realize I have licked my lips more than once, but I call out, "Managed it without licking my lips!" and she calls back, "No way! Well done!" and I smile because I love praise from my mom.

When the door buzzer goes, my stomach plunges. I know it's Chris, because Rosie would just run down from her apartment and knock. I'm sitting on my bed doing my homework, but I get up to close my door. I don't want to see him. Mom's spent ages getting ready: redoing all her makeup and changing outfits at least three times.

I hear voices in our hallway and kissing noises, which make me want to throw up. Then I hear Chris's voice saying, "What do you mean, she's not here yet?"

Mom murmurs something. Chris says, "Yeah, but you told her seven, right? She's never on time, that girl."

There's another word in between "that" and "girl" which I don't like hearing because it's rude and Chris says it far too often. Mom says something in a consoling voice. Chris says clearly, "No, I don't want a drink here. I've had a day from hell and I just want to get out and relax." That's another thing I don't like about him: He's too loud.

I don't really want to listen but I can't avoid it when they're just outside my room. Mom says something, and then I hear movement and footsteps on the stairs outside the apartment, and I'm guessing she's gone up to find Rosie.

Chris huffs and shuffles around in the hallway for a moment. Then my door opens, making me jump. He's so rude he didn't even knock before opening my door.

His face appears. It's kind of thin and weasely, like Filch from Harry Potter. His nose is too big, and his eyes are too small. His head doesn't suit the rest of his body, which is sort of stocky. It's like his head has shrunk, which would explain the size of his brain. "Hey, Jelly," he says, staring at me.

"Hi, Chris," I say, and then look back down at my homework.

Chris comes in (uninvited, naturally) and stands on my rug, hands in his pockets, looking around. The room suddenly feels a whole lot smaller. "You still have a poster of My Little Pony on your wall?" he says. "At your age?"

My face flames red. That poster has been there for

about four years. It's got a lot of good memories for me.

"You should be into boy bands and short shorts and all that stuff," he says, his gaze sweeping my room.

I don't know what to say to him. He's standing in between me and the door, and it feels like I'm trapped.

"Maybe not short shorts," he adds, glancing at my legs. "Not got your mom's figure."

To my utter relief at this moment, Mom comes back. "Hey!" she says brightly, standing in my doorway. "Rosie's on her way right now."

There are more footsteps on the stairs and I hear the faint sound of music from Rosie's earphones. She turns the volume up way further than you're supposed to.

"About time," says Chris, and he turns and goes, leaving my door wide open. The tinny music heads into the living room.

Mom comes in and gives me a hug. "Don't stay up too late," she says. "School night."

I hug her back tightly. For a moment I don't think I can let go, but then she pulls away and I nod and smile like I always do. Option Two: smile.

The door to the apartment clicks shut, and Option Two slides off my face, leaving a frown in its place.

Chapter 4

I try to get back to my homework, but there's a kind of hole inside me, like when something is taken away and you miss it and so you want to fill it up with something else.

My Secret Power

I have a secret power
It lives inside my hands
It's deadlier than spiders
and follows my commands

It burns right through your eyeballs
It suffocates your lungs
It stops your heart and brain
                    and blood
It rips away your tongue

So when you next insult me
Or disappoint my mom
Just think what I can do to you
You PUTRID
       RED-FACED
       SCUM

I wish I did have a secret power. But even after writing the poem, I still feel like there's something missing, so I wander out to the living room. Rosie is where I expected her to be, on the sofa, eyes glued to her phone, swiping the screen this way and that. She still has her earphones in, so I go over and tap her on the shoulder. She jumps a mile and swears.

"Don't *do* that! You nearly gave me a heart attack!" She pulls out an earbud.

"Sorry," I say. "What are you doing?"

"Beautifying myself," she says. "Look."

I sit next to her on the sofa and she shows me her screen. It's a photo of a really pretty girl. "Who's that?" I ask.

Rosie giggles. "It's me."

"What?"

"It's an app. I'll show you." She flips through the options. You take a selfie, and then you can choose how to edit the photo. You can change eye color, make your cheeks slimmer, lips redder, eyes bigger. "Let's do you," she says, and snaps a photo of me before I've had a chance to think about it. "What shall we change?" she says, her fingers flying over the screen.

Before my eyes, my face is turned into something,

someone . . . else. Rosie holds up the phone to me. "See?" she says, smiling. "You look gorgeous!"

I stare at the photo, mesmerized. The girl in the picture is thinner than me. Her face isn't so round, and her muddy green eyes have been brightened. Her lips are a pale pink and her hair has been thickened to fall in a wave across her forehead. She—I—*it*—looks like a Disney princess. "Wow," I manage to say.

"Now *there's* a supermodel face," says Rosie, admiring her own work. "There's another app that'll do your whole body. I'll show you what I did to mine."

Within seconds I'm looking at a picture of Rosie in a bikini, her legs long and tanned. She looks like those girls in perfume or magazine ads. "Stand up and I'll do you," she says enthusiastically.

"No!" I say, and it comes out more sharply than I intended. "No, I—that's all right, I'm fine. Really. Do another one of you."

She obliges, and I watch her turn her own image into something you might see on a bus stop ad or the side of a building. Smooth and thin and perfect, just like all the other smooth and thin and perfect women and girls I see everywhere. "Do you wish you looked like that?" I ask, but even as I say it, I know it's a dumb question.

"Yeah, of course," she says, not even glancing up. "Who wouldn't?"

Later, in bed, I stare at the wall. I can't stop seeing that image of my altered face, the one Rosie said was "gorgeous." It was. It looked amazing. I do wish I looked like that, of course I do. Except—it's not real. A computer changed my face into something I couldn't ever look like. Something *no one* could ever look like.

Staring

I stare at the wall
It is smooth
           white
                unbroken
But under the surface
there are bricks
        ugly
            lumpy
                 hard-edged
And cement, holding them in place
making sure the wall doesn't fall down
So the smooth, white, unbroken-ness
is not the whole wall
People like smooth
              white
                   unbroken things
As long as you don't show them
             what's underneath

24

Chapter 5

The next morning is Friday and Mom is puffy-eyed and yawning at breakfast.

"Did you have a good night?" I ask.

"Oh, it was all right. Just a bit . . . well, a bit . . . I dunno." She shrugs.

"A bit what?" I ask, pouring out a helping of Cocoa Krispies.

She comes to sit with me, mug of green tea in hand. "It's nothing really. We went down to the King's Arms and there were some of Chris's friends there. I mean, I didn't *mind* that they were there, of course I didn't. They were all talking about some trip they'd been on together years ago, and how their soccer teams were doing, and so Chris mostly talked to them. . . ." She stops for a moment. "There wasn't much I could join in with, that's all. But, you know, I was happy just to be there."

She doesn't sound that happy about it.

"I listened to the band mostly," she goes on, looking a little more cheerful.

"Band?" I say.

"Yeah, they've started having live music. They played all kinds of things—a couple of covers, and some original stuff. It was nice." She smiles. "There was this song about a dog—"

"A *dog*?" I ask. "In a *pop* song?"

Mom laughs. "No, it was more like a kind of ballad. It was about this dog who met a man and they became friends, and the dog trained the man to do everything he wanted. It was really clever." Her face becomes more thoughtful. "And then there was this bit toward the end of the song where the man started to neglect the dog, and then one day he didn't come back, and the dog was just left, waiting. . . ."

I stare at her. "Wow. That's . . . really sad." I don't say it, but the song sounds completely weird to me, and not the kind of thing she'd usually go for at all. Mom likes songs about girls getting revenge after they've been dumped.

She stares over toward the sofa, as though seeing last night's view. "It was so cleverly done, you know? Really subtle. Kind of drew you in and then—*wham*!—hit you with the sad bit." She curls her hands around the mug. "I really liked it. And the singer's voice . . . he drew you in too. And then I got a bit of a headache, so I came home."

"I didn't hear you come in," I say. Chris's voice usually wakes me up.

"I came back on my own. Chris went on to a club with his friends."

I'm not an expert on boyfriends, but that doesn't sound very nice to me. Taking your girlfriend out for the evening, then ignoring her and making her walk home by herself? I bite my lip so that I don't say so out loud.

My mom deserves better.

Chapter 6

As I walk to school, I feel kind of sad inside. It's not that I want a dad. My own dad walked out so many years ago that I don't even remember him. But I wish Mom had a boyfriend who made her happy.

The playground is full of kids and their parents. It's a great place to watch people. If you want to be good at impressions, you have to study how they walk, how they hold their heads while they talk, whether they wave their hands around. Some people have really expressive faces—they're the best ones to copy. It's almost impossible not to show *something* on your face. A person who talks without smiling or raising their eyebrows is really unusual—try it and you'll see. Emma Ojobe's dad is like that. I did an impression of him once to Emma and she said it was dead scary and I had to promise to never do it again.

"Jelly!" Kayma comes running up. "Hey, look what I got." She holds out a hand and I see tiny sparkly gems on each fingernail.

"Nice!" I say. I can see from one glance that they're gel nails, professionally applied. I know because Mom has them too.

"I went to the manicurist with Fliss," says Kayma. Fliss is her much older sister who works in a coffee shop. "You should come with us next time."

Kayma's fingers are long and slim. My fingers are wide and my nails are kind of square. I wiggle them at Kayma and say in a fake Southern accent, "Ain't no nail product alive that can make these fingers look cute, baby!"

She laughs and drops into the same accent. "You just don't think enough of yourself, honey. You trust the manicurist. The manicurist *knows*."

We giggle. Her accent isn't as good as mine, but that's OK because it's fun and silly and we've been doing fake accents for years, ever since we started watching *My Little Pony*. For the whole time we were in second grade, she was Rarity and I was Pinkie Pie. That's when I got the poster on my wall.

Sanvi comes to join us and says, "Kayma, can we talk about The K Factor?"

"I've got *loads* of ideas!" says Kayma. "Like, we could do a song, or a mime, or write a sketch, or do some gymnastics—"

Sanvi looks horrified. "I can't even do a cartwheel! What about dancing?" She does Indian dancing on Saturdays and she's really good at it.

"Dancing, me?! You must be joking," says Kayma. Sanvi's face falls.

The sun is out today, and our classroom windows are big. As the morning hours pass, I can feel my skirt sticking to my legs. Lunch is macaroni and cheese, and I eat every last scrap. My tummy feels wobbly, not because of the food but because after lunch it's PE.

I love PE. I love running around outside—I'm strong and fast and have good ball skills—but something has to happen before and after PE, and that's the bit I hate.

Mr. Lenck finishes taking attendance, and then Ms. Jones comes in. She has a round face with widely spaced eyes and a very straight, quite long nose. She smells of something orangey and she always wears sneakers with neon laces. "Right, class!" she says, and her voice is slightly too high and slightly too loud all the time because she's so used to shouting outside that she forgets to talk normally. "Let's go!" Up until last year, we all had to change in the same classroom, boys and girls. I hated it. I felt as if everyone was looking at me, at the soft rolls that hang over my waistband. This year the boys change in the classroom but the girls go down to the end of the corridor. It's better but I still hate it because the other girls . . . well, they don't look like me. All those thin bodies, those skinny legs . . . they make me hot and humiliated, and even though the girls don't say anything, I know—I just *know*—what they're thinking when they see me: *I'm glad I don't look like that.*

don't look

don't look

don't see me

don't see what's under the layers

don't let your eyes widen in horror

don't let your nose wrinkle in disgust

don't see my skin

don't see my blubber

don't see my insides on my outsides

don't look

It's soccer today. I'm good at soccer because I'm fast and I can control the ball. Verity Hughes picks me to be on her team, and we pull on the red pinnies while the opposing team takes the yellow. The pinnies have been used for years—everything at this school is falling apart—and the elastic at the bottom of mine has long since given up any stretchiness. "Look," I say, sticking my thumbs under the hem and holding it out, "my elastic is dead!"

"Just as well!" Verity grins at me. "It would've cut you in half."

I laugh with her. Verity is one of the whitest, skinniest, and smoothest girls in class.

Ms. Jones sends the red and yellow teams to the far corner of the field. Will Matsunaga is wearing yellow and calls out to me before we start, "Gonna take you *down*, Waters!"

"You wish!" I retort, and the game starts. Verity is terrible at soccer, she kicks hard but has no direction control, so quite often we lose a throw-in to the other team, which makes me really annoyed. It's not long before we're down three–nil, and Will is crowing like a big fat crow that's found roadkill to chomp on. "Told you, Waters!"

I boot the ball over his head toward the goal—too high. You shouldn't kick in anger, you lose your technique. The ball flies about nine feet over the crossbar and plops down into another match, causing shouts of protest. "Sorry!" I yell. "Don't know my own strength!"

Will shakes his head, teasing. "You're like the Hulk, Jelly. He lets his anger get the better of him too."

"I'm not angry," I say angrily. The ball comes flying back through the air without warning. I twist in surprise and fall, sitting awkwardly on my own foot and bruising my backside. Will bursts into raucous laughter.

"You OK?" Verity offers me a hand up, though I can see she's laughing too.

"I'm fine," I say, blinking back tears of pain. I get to my feet and take Option Two again. "Did you *see* that? I was like a hippo falling off a cliff!" I demonstrate the action and fall heavily, deliberately, on my own foot again. The others laugh, and something twinges painfully inside me, but I keep going because they're laughing, and if they're laughing then they like me, and that's what I want.

Ms. Jones comes over to see what's going on. "I might have known it was your team," she says to me. "Angelica, you're very funny, but this is supposed to be a game."

"Oh, don't worry, miss," Will assures her. "We're wiping the floor with them. Three–nil so far."

Ms. Jones glances at Verity. "Are you remembering to use the passing techniques we practiced?"

"Yes, miss," lies Verity, who hasn't passed the ball to anyone yet.

"Well, we've only got five minutes left, so I'll watch you. Who's got the ball?"

For the last five minutes of the lesson there's no messing about, and because Ms. Jones is watching, Verity focuses better. In a miraculous moment she passes the ball to me, and I boot it clear past Safira into the goal. "Yesss!" I do the airplane, running around the field.

The final score is three–two to Will's team, but my header into the top-left corner of the net in the last seconds is a thing of beauty. "You should be on the school team," Will says to me as Ms. Jones blows the whistle.

She hears him. "That's a good point, Angelica—why haven't you tried out for the under-twelves?"

For a moment, I am filled with pride. But . . . surely no one wants a Heffalump like me playing for the school. I imagine the snickers from opposing teams if I were to turn up on the team bus. . . . I am the girl who doesn't fit into the elasticated pinnies after all.

"Well," I say, "if you want someone to fall on their butt, I'm *really* good at that."

Ms. Jones shakes her head. "If you took things a little more seriously, you could be an excellent player, Angelica." She calls out to everyone, "Time to get changed!"

And then it's the ordeal of getting back into school clothes, and this time it's worse because I'm feeling all weird and self-conscious from the compliment a minute ago. As I change, I keep my red face turned toward the rows of pegs with their oversized PE bags and smelly lunch boxes piled up underneath.

SMELLS

Everything is smelly
a yogurt pot, a welly

The cured meat in the deli
The beef strips, the pork belly

But nothing is as smelly
as a sweating
       pig-like

       Jelly

Chapter 7

Getting home on a Friday always feels like such a relief. I did it! Another week is over and I made it through and people still like me! So despite the PE changing hell, I feel good as I walk home. I like weekends.

I'm humming when I run up the stairs to our door, but as soon as I go in I see a man's jacket hanging on the rack, and I stop dead. Chris's jacket has a very particular smell: dirt and engine oil, because he likes to do motocross, which is a really dangerous form of motorbike racing. The smell makes me feel queasy. I wasn't expecting him to be here today, especially after he left Mom to walk home on her own last night, and a kind of cold fury rushes through me. I was feeling good, and now he's spoiled it!

There are noises coming from my mom's bedroom, and they are the kind of kissing noises I don't want to hear. The door behind me is still open. Mom's handbag is hanging from the coatrack.

Before I even know what I'm doing, I'm reaching into her bag, taking out her purse, and removing a ten-dollar bill. Then I pull the door closed very gently so that no one will know I was ever here.

If I have to waste an hour in a coffee shop because of Mom's stupid boyfriend, she can buy my milkshake and chocolate brownie.

Kayma's sister Fliss is working in the coffee shop today. There are two coffee shops within walking distance of my apartment, but this one is nicer. It's called Coffeetastic, which is a terrible name for a shop but it's always busy because their coffee is cheaper than the big chains. Also, the owners did it up with all this red leather and chrome so it looks like an authentic diner, which makes it cool. There's even a neon sign in the window where the name "Coffeetastic" glows green at night.

Fliss gives me a huge grin when I come in. She's the spitting image of Kayma, only five years older. Their younger sister Hula looks identical too. It's like the three of them are clones. "Jelly! So cool to see you! You on your own?"

"Yeah," I say, and the word hurts but I smile.

"What can I get you?" Fliss asks. "We've got some squillionaire's shortbread. It's like millionaire's, only it's got extra layers of chocolate and toffee pieces."

"Mmm." I lick my lips. "That'll ruin my diet."

"You're on a *diet*?" Fliss says, her eyes opening very wide. "You're kidding me! You're gorgeous!"

I break into a Southern accent. "Why, honey, ain't that *precious* of you to say so! Ah don't know *what* you mean. Ah only spend *two hours* getting ready every morning. Ah practically *roll* out of bed looking like this!"

Fliss laughs. "You're so good at that. Straight out of those reality shows. You should be on TV." She slides a large slice of the shortbread onto a shiny white plate. "What do you want to go with this? Iced choco-caramel whippy?"

"Iced who now?"

"Trust me." She pours milk in a jug and starts adding various ingredients. "You try this—if you don't like it,

I'll give you your money back. It'll blow your mind."

I pay with Mom's tenner and take my tray over to the only table that's free. It still has the previous customer's trash on it. Why can't people tidy up after themselves? Grumpily I dump my bags on the floor and put my own drink and cake on the table. Then I pile the leftover plates and cups onto the tray and take it to the disposal area. When I come back a man is standing by my table, looking at it hopefully. He's holding a latte in one hand and a guitar case in the other. The guitar is causing a bit of a problem because of the baby stroller at the next table.

"Excuse me," I say to the man, trying to wriggle past him. "That's my table."

"Dammit," he says. "I was hoping you'd been called away on an urgent matter and I could nab it."

"Sorry." I sit down. The man sighs and rotates three hundred and sixty degrees, looking to see if there are any other tables available. There aren't.

I sigh too because now I feel obliged to offer. "You can have the other chair, if you like," I say in a voice that sounds more inviting than I feel.

"Are you sure?" he asks. "I don't want to make you uncomfortable."

I look at him properly. He's tall, kind of hunched over in that way tall people can be when they realize everyone around them is shorter, so they stoop a bit so that they don't stick out so much. Dark, slightly curly hair with tanned and freckly skin. His eyes are brown and look kind, and his voice is quite deep. He's wearing a thin shirt and a brown leather jacket that's scuffed at the edges. He reminds me of Mr. Collery, who used to teach me in second grade and was really nice.

Unlike Chris's, the stranger's head is the right size for the rest of him.

"It's OK," I say.

"Well, thank you," he says, and puts his latte on the table. Then he maneuvres his guitar case around so that it's vertical and sticking up between his knees as he sits. It makes me laugh a bit. "I know," he says. "Not exactly convenient to carry around. Can't put it in my pocket like a harmonica."

"A what?"

"You don't know what a harmonica is?" He raises his eyes to the ceiling. "What do they teach kids at school these days?"

"Multiplication tables," I tell him. "And expanded noun phrases."

Now it was his turn to stare. "What in heaven's name are those?"

"Oh, well . . ." I can't resist. I straighten my back and lower my head a little. Under the table, I twitch my feet so that the toes are pointing inward. Mr. Lenck's voice comes out of my mouth: "A noun phrase is a phrase that contains a noun. When you expand it, you add more adjectives to make it more interesting. So, 'The girl sat at a table' might become 'A bubbly, cheerful girl sat at a shiny round table.' Expanding the phrase makes the writing more interesting."

The man smiles at me. "Who's that then?"

"My teacher, Mr. Lenck," I say, relaxing out of the impression and slouching again. "He always talks like that."

"Does he sniff a lot too?"

"Yeah, all the time. We should design him a tissue that hangs from his nose." Ooh, I like that idea. Must remember it for a future impression.

"School has changed a lot since I was there," the man says. "It sounds more boring. And if they don't teach you about harmonicas, then I can't see the point of expanded whatnots." He reaches into his jacket pocket and pulls out a small rectangular object. According to my math lessons, I should call it a small cuboid. Which, in case you're interested, has twelve edges, eight vertices, and six faces. Briefly I consider doing an impression of Mr. Lenck explaining this, but I decide not to. The poor stranger doesn't deserve it.

The man lifts the cuboid (seriously, does anyone actually use that word?) to his lips and blows—and it makes a sound, a bit like a tinny sort of trumpet. He plays a run of notes on it. The people at the next table turn around to frown, which delights me because usually *I'm* the one being frowned at by grown-ups. "This is a harmonica," the man says, holding it out for me to see. "It's a small musical instrument. Pretty useful. You can play tunes and chords on it, and it's very popular in blues and country music."

"Oh," I say. "That's kind of cool."

He looks pleased as he tucks it back into his pocket. "It's a very underestimated instrument. You should check it out on YouTube. Have a look at Sonny Boy Williamson. And Stevie Wonder."

"OK." I take a bite of the squillionaire's shortbread and nearly die, it's that good. "Oh my *gosh*."

He smiles. "That looks tasty."

I can't speak. If you try to talk while eating

shortbread, you inhale crumbs and choke. I'm always starving after school, and the squillionaire is soon an ex-squillionaire. The caramel whippy-shake, or whatever it is, is delicious (so I won't be asking for my money back), and the horrid feeling in my tummy caused by finding Chris at home starts to go away.

The woman at the next table with the stroller gets up. The man at my table has to squeeze in tightly so she can get the stroller out. "Thanks," she says to him. "I don't know—they should make these things smaller! I got stuck in a door the other day! It's like they think moms don't go anywhere!"

I prick up my ears at her voice. It's quite distinctive and her lip does a funny thing whenever she says the "m" sound. Without even thinking, I start to make the same shape with my mouth as the door swings shut behind her.

The man glances behind him at the now-empty table. "I could move across now, if you like. Give you more room."

"I don't know," I say in the woman's voice. "You'd think they'd make tables smaller, so that people didn't have to squash up so much! In fact, they should just get rid of tables, so that we don't have this problem at all!"

The man's eyebrows shoot up in delighted surprise. "That's *very* good," he says admiringly. "That's just like her! You've got a great ear for voices, haven't you?"

I shrug, smiling. "I like doing impressions. I'm entering my school talent show."

"Well," he says, "I bet you'll win." He moves across to the free table, takes out his phone, and begins scrolling through something on the screen, his eyes flicking from left to right as he reads. I wipe condensation off the sides of my drink and look out the window. People wander past, some quickly, some slowly. All the high schools are out, so bunches of teenagers are hanging around, shouting, jostling, and checking their phones. The girls roll their skirts up at the waist so that their long skinny legs are on show. The boys have their pants hanging loose at the waist so you can see the tops of their underpants. Fashion is weird.

All those people, those happy-looking people. I bet they don't go home and write terrible poetry because they feel they don't fit in anywhere. Why does everyone else have it figured out and I don't?

People-watching

I sit in the window
        and watch them go by.
They shout and they giggle,
        they smile and they cry
Behind all this glass
        I am not in that world
My hands round my teacup
        are tightly curled
And what's so bizarre
        is that when I step out
And go through that door
        I am stricken with doubt
Cos though I am sure
        I've gone into the day
I've never felt further away

"Bye then."

The voice jerks me back to the coffee shop. The man with the guitar and the harmonica is standing by my table. His latte glass is empty, apart from the frothy bits of beige milk that cling to the sides like tiny clouds.

"Oh!" I say. "Bye."

He smiles at me. "Keep practicing that gift of yours. And don't forget the harmonica players: Sonny Boy Williamson and Stevie Wonder."

"I won't. Thanks."

He goes, deftly maneuvering around anyone coming into the shop and ensuring that nothing bangs into his guitar case. I'd like to play guitar. I don't play any musical instruments. When my friends started to learn clarinet and violin at the age of seven, Mom didn't have any spare money. Now her business is doing well, maybe I could ask for guitar lessons.

More and more people come into the coffee shop, and my plate and mug are empty. Reluctantly I squeeze out of the too-small space I somehow got myself into, pick up my bags, and take my tray to the disposal area. I want to say goodbye to Fliss, but she's busy creating three different smoothies for the teenage girls who've just come in, so after hesitating a moment I head out of the shop.

It's been about forty minutes since I left the apartment, so it should be safe to go back. I walk slowly, dragging my PE bag along the pavement even though I know it scuffs the fabric.

As I unlock my front door, I see the same jacket hanging on the coatrack and smell the same smell. He's still here. I feel a bit sick, but I take a breath and call in my this-is-normal voice, "I'm back!"

Chapter 8

"Hey, darling!" Mom's voice comes from the bathroom. "With you in a minute! Chris is here."

"OK," I call back, when it's anything but OK.

I go into the living room and dump my bags by the table. Chris is sprawled in the armchair, flicking through channels on the TV with the remote. He looks up. "You alright?" He turns back to the TV.

"Yeah," I lie.

Mom comes in in a waft of shower gel. She's all flushed and pink, wearing a strappy top, thin swishy skirt, and no shoes. "Hello, gorgeous," she says, giving me a hug.

Chris gives a kind of snort and, not taking his eyes from the TV, mutters, "No one would guess you two were related."

Mom is gorgeous. So I know what Chris is saying, and it stings.

Mom gives a kind of tinkly laugh and cups my face. "It's just puppy fat," she says to Chris while smiling at me. "When she hits her teens, she'll lengthen out. You'll see."

I smile back at her, trying to scrub the words "puppy fat" from my brain.

A frown flits across her face and she glances at the clock. "Aren't you back later than usual? Was there something happening after school?"

I can't tell her about the coffee shop. She might ask how I had enough money, and then I'd have to lie or she'd know I'd been in the apartment earlier.

"Yeah," I say, and overelaborate as usual. "Miss Keegan asked me and Kayma to help her reshelve the library books at the end of class, and there were way more than we thought, and the next thing we know Mr. Harding is coming along and is all like, 'What are you still doing here? I need to get up in the ceiling to fix one of these lights,' and Miss Keegan was all, 'Oh no, girls, I'm so sorry, the clock's not working and I just lost track of time!' and Mr. Harding was like, 'So now the flipping clock isn't working and no one told me. These things are meant to be reported!' and Miss Keegan went all pale and fluttery and said it wasn't her fault and then—" I take a breath "—we go out the usual way but the school gates were already locked so we had to come back in again and go out through the office. Sorry, I should have texted." This is a safe lie because there's no way Mom will check on it.

Chris gives an exaggerated sigh of boredom and turns up the volume on the TV.

"Well, that's worth staying for," Mom says, amused. "Don't worry. I got caught up in something myself."

I say nothing.

"I thought we might get Chinese this evening," she goes on, "since Chris is here."

"Is he staying over?" I say, glancing in his direction. Mom laughs, sounding embarrassed, and turns away. "Oh, I don't know. We haven't thought that far ahead. Want a cup of tea?"

I follow her into the kitchen. "Aren't you still angry with him about last night?" I say in a low voice.

She does that fake tinkly laugh again. "Angry? I wasn't angry, love."

"He made you walk home on your own," I remind her.

"He didn't *make* me," she corrects me, switching on the kettle. "I chose to walk home by myself. Honestly, Jelly, you're making a mountain out of a molehill!"

Her voice is sharp, and I feel properly told off. Shame swirls in my stomach. I shouldn't have said anything. Desperate to put it right, I say, "Hey, I've got a new joke! Knock, knock!"

Mom sighs and says, "Who's there?"

"Ya."

"Ya who?"

"Aww, I'm excited to see you too!"

Mom pauses for a moment while she figures it out and then smiles in a small way, the type of smile that doesn't reach her eyes. "Very good."

I feel anxious. The joke wasn't good enough. "Try this one: Knock, knock."

"Jelly . . ."

"Come on," I urge.

"Who's there?"

"Scold."

"Scold who?"

"Scold outside, let me in!"

She nods. "That one's good too."

"I've got another one—"

"*No*, Jelly. Not now. Why don't you go and look at the take-out menu?"

I ate squillionaire's shortbread only an hour ago, but my stomach feels hollow. When the order arrives, I eat way too much food.

Later, much later, I go to my room and to my book.

Puppy Fat

Fat puppies are cute
all fluffy and round
They sit up and beg
They roll on the gound.

Fat people are lazy
Fat people are bad
They're told so on TV
They're meant to be sad

So don't call me puppy
When you mean my size
Cos puppies are cute
and I'm otherwise

I am woken in the morning by the sound of the apartment door slamming, and Mom crying. I stare at the ceiling and feel the churn of last night's supper in my stomach. Then I get up and go to her room.

She's sitting on the side of the bed in her nightie, head in her hands, shaking. I sit next to her and put my arm around her. She gives a huge sniff and reaches for a tissue to wipe her face. "Oh, sweetie. Sorry. Did I wake you up?"

"No," I lie. "What's the matter?"

"Oh . . ." She draws a shaky breath and stares at the carpet. "He's left me, that's all." She shrugs. "I mean, I was kind of expecting it. He says I'm no fun anymore. I text him too much. And he doesn't want to be tied down."

"Tied down?"

"He thinks I'm trying to trap him into marriage or something." Her eyes overflow again. "I always mess up. Even when I was a kid, I couldn't do anything right! I guess I should be used to it by now." She bites her lip for a moment. "Back to being just us two again."

"I like it that way," I tell her. "Two is the perfect number."

She kisses me on the top of my head. "I'd better get in the shower," she says.

I sit on her bed for a few moments longer. I'm sad for Mom of course. I hate seeing her upset. But I'm relieved that Chris won't be coming around anymore. I didn't like him, and he wasn't nice to Mom. I don't understand why anyone *wouldn't* want Mom as a girlfriend. She's kind and a great mom, and she's so beautiful. When she smiles—a real, heartfelt, deep-inside smile—it reaches right up into her eyes and they sparkle and shine. It warms me: It makes me feel good.

Mom would say beauty is mascara and high heels and nice hair and skinny pants. She works for a beauty company so I guess she'd know.

But I'd say that beauty is eyes that sparkle when you smile.

Chapter 9

It's Sunday afternoon, and Sanvi and I are in Kayma's bedroom. Kayma lives in a duplex, with four bedrooms and a big kitchen/dining room downstairs, as well as a sitting room. Fliss, Kayma, and Hula have a bedroom each, which makes their house feel HUGE to me. Hula is sweet but kind of annoying because she always wants to be doing whatever Kayma's doing, and she's two whole years younger. Kayma hates her tagging along. Today she's coloring a "HULA KEEP OUT" sign to go on her bedroom door.

I feel a bit bad to have left Mom at home on her own, but she said she was going to catch up on work anyway.

She spent yesterday sending hundreds of texts, though she said none of them were to Chris. I hope that's true. She also spent an hour and a half on the phone talking to Cass from work, though I'm not sure it made her feel any better because she drank three cups of green tea when she'd finished.

"Why don't we do the same comedy characters we did last year?" Kayma suggests, and I drag my attention back to the present. She and Sanvi are trying to decide on their act for The K Factor. "We could do a new sketch."

"We can't do it without Jelly," objects Sanvi. "And besides, Mrs. Belize didn't like it."

Last year our sketch centered around the three of us dressed up in wigs and old people's clothes, trying to buy things in a store and not understanding the answers. Mrs. Belize said she felt we were stereotyping the elderly and it wasn't kind. But Kayma pointed out that her great-granny was *exactly* like the character she was playing, and so Mrs. Belize had to admit defeat. Especially as Kayma's great-granny was actually in the audience and laughed her head off. And Mrs. Belize's daughter Julie, the "special guest judge," said we showed "enormous talent in acting ability and comic timing."

"What about a song?" I suggest.

Sanvi bites her lip. "I dunno. I get really nervous about singing."

"You've got a really nice voice," I tell her. "You could totally do a song. Kayma could do the first verse and you could do the second, and you could sing the choruses together."

Sanvi looks shyly at me. "You think I've got a nice voice?"

"Course I do," I tell her. "Remember you got that solo in one of the Christmas carols last year? It sounded amazing."

"Yes, but I puked beforehand," Sanvi points out, "because I was so scared."

"But you still sang it," I say. "So I bet you could do it again."

"We could design our own outfits too," Kayma says, tossing over a heavy magazine from beside her. "Look at these."

The magazine is so thick it makes a *thomp* noise as it lands. "Vogooey?" I say, trying to pronounce the title.

"*Vogue*," says Kayma. "Like, to rhyme with . . . um . . . rogue. Fliss didn't want it anymore. She gave me a whole pile of stuff. She used to buy fashion mags all the time."

Sanvi and I flick through the pages. The magazine is

full of pictures of women wearing weird outfits. Some of them are truly bizarre.

"Why would you want an entirely see-through dress?" I exclaim. "I mean, why would you want the whole world to see your . . . bits?"

Sanvi giggles. "Can you imagine wearing that out to the shopping center?"

Other outfits just look boring. Gray sweaters that hang shapelessly. Black leggings that look just like the ones you can buy in practically any clothes store ever. Only they cost . . . "*Two hundred and fifty-nine dollars?!*" I say in astonishment. "For *leggings*?"

"It's cause they're designer, isn't it?" says Kayma.

"They're five dollars at Walmart!" I protest.

Sanvi flicks through more pages. "Not many Indian girls."

"Or black ones," says Kayma.

"Or fat ones," I add. "None, in fact. Everyone is thin, thin, thin." I turn the pages, noticing my fingers, square and chunky. These clothes . . . they're not for me. Nothing about this world is for me. Fashion is for skinny people. And people with a *lot* of money. Even if I *had* two hundred and fifty-nine dollars, I wouldn't spend it on a pair of pants. They're just *pants*, after all. Two hundred and fifty-nine dollars could get you a vacation. Or horse-riding lessons. Or a year's supply of Kit Kats. I stare at the skinny ladies. I bet they never get to eat a Kit Kat. They're missing out. Kit Kats are one of the joys in life.

"I've got loads," Kayma says, sliding over a pile of the thick magazines. "Dunno what to do with them."

"Burn them," I say helpfully.

"We could make a collage," Sanvi says. "Maybe."

I tip over the pile. They make a waterfall of *thomp*s on the carpet. "What's this?" Tucked between the magazines is a slim paperback titled *Your Body and Its Changes*. A cartoon girl stands on the front, hands on hips, confident.

Kayma wriggles across the floor to have a look. Then she lets out a giggle. "Ohh! *I* know this book! Fliss had it on her shelves, and I used to sneak a peek at it every now and then. It's full of rude stuff!"

"Rude stuff?" I ask, intrigued, and open it to a random page. There's a diagram of something that looks vaguely like a lake with two rivers running into it and an opening to the sea. I read the description underneath: *The female reproductive system*. "What the what?"

"I remember that," Sanvi says. "We did that last year."

"We did?" I stare at the picture. "Ohh . . . right! Yeah, I think I remember it. Ms. Jones showed us that video about babies and told us all off for being silly."

Kayma laughs. "That was sooo embarrassing. And they kept saying . . . *certain words* in the video."

Sanvi is going very red in the face. "It wasn't nice," she says primly. "It was private stuff, we shouldn't have had a lesson on it like that."

"Toss me the book," Kayma says. "I want to dare Jelly."

You can't turn down a dare, especially when it's from your best friends. "What kind of dare?" I ask apprehensively.

She flips through the pages and then hands back the open book. "Dare you to read this bit aloud in the voice of that guy who narrates those stuffy nature specials—Attinbury."

"Attenborough," I correct her. I look down at the page, titled *Periods*. "Oh, Kayma, nooo!"

"Dare!"

I clear my throat and prepare my best David Attenborough voice. "Once a month, the lining of the womb thickens in preparation for an egg. If no egg implants, then the lining breaks down and travels down the vagina, emerging as blood. This is called a period."

Kayma is laughing so hard she's crying. "You said . . . *vagina*," she splutters.

Sanvi is wriggling in embarrassment. "Stop, please stop!"

"You have to *know* about them," I tease her.

"You can't *not* know in this house," Kayma says, wiping her eyes and calming down. "I always know when Fliss has hers because she gets really grumpy and mean. And the bathroom is full of plastic packets, and once the toilet didn't flush properly and . . . ugh!"

"I don't want them," Sanvi says, looking pale. "Periods. Ew. Yuck. I feel sick."

"You might not get them for years," Kayma says.

"Maybe you could have all those bits taken out," I suggest.

"But then she couldn't have a baby," Kayma points out.

"I do want a baby," Sanvi says. "When I'm grown-up."

"*I* don't," I say firmly.

Sanvi looks shocked. "What, never?"

"Nope."

"That's sad," says Sanvi.

"No, it isn't," I retort. "If I don't want one, I shouldn't have to have one."

"I've finished this," Kayma interrupts, holding up her poster. "HULA KEEP OUT" is bright and bold and no one could miss it. "Just need to put it on my door." She gets up and opens her bedroom door.

Hula falls into the room. "*What*?" she says, before anyone has a chance to say anything. "I wasn't *listening*."

"You so were!" cries Kayma. She shouts downstairs, "Mooom! Hula's been listening at my door again!"

There's no answer from downstairs.

"I *wasn't* listening," Hula insists. She giggles. "Are you going to have *babies*?"

"*Mooom!*" Kayma yells even louder. "Hula won't leave us alone!"

"Let your little sister join in!" comes the shout from downstairs. Kayma's face darkens with anger.

Hula grins at Kayma. "Mom says you have to."

"No way!"

Hula gets down on her knees on the carpet. "Pleeeease," she says, making her eyes big and round, and holding up her hand like she's praying. Hula only has one hand because years ago she was in a car accident with Kayma's dad. A truck drove into his car and he died. Hula was in the back in a car seat and survived, but her arm was crushed and they had to cut it off at the elbow. Having only half an arm doesn't stop her being annoying though. And Kayma's mom always seems to take Hula's side.

"No," says Kayma. She pushes Hula out and shuts the door in her face.

There is a wail as Hula bursts into tears on the other side, followed by footsteps running down the stairs. Then a moment later there's a shout from Kayma's mom: "KAYMA, GET DOWN HERE RIGHT NOW. I WANT A WORD WITH YOU."

Kayma sighs heavily. "Here we go again." She tugs open the door and turns to look at the two of us. "Next time we go to someone else's house, OK?"

Chapter 10

"Why would anyone spend that much money on leggings?" I muse a few days later, watching Mom slice open the top of a large cardboard box which arrived for her: the latest delivery of makeup. "I still can't understand it. They were just leggings."

"*Designer* leggings," Mom says. "You're paying for the name and the style. The line of a dress, the cut of a pair of pants . . . the difference between comfort and elegance." She starts lifting out boxes of eye shadow, powder compacts, and pencils. Everything in the cardboard box is slim and shiny.

I watch her slim fingers carefully place the slim products in neat piles.

"I'll never be elegant," I say gloomily.

Mom says absently, "Of course you will. I'll help you. You'll turn heads, sweetheart."

I already do, I think, *but not for the right reasons*. A tiny frown flickers across her forehead and she leans over to me. "Are you getting a pimple on your nose?"

Instinctively I feel the bridge of my nose. There is a small lump there. It's sore. "Oh, nooo," I moan.

"You had one on your chin the other week, didn't you?" Mom says. "Poor love. That's what growing up does to you." She rummages in the box. "I've got something that'll fix it up in a flash. Hang on . . ." She pulls out a tiny tube. "Vanish gel. It's magic stuff."

"Thanks," I say. I have a kind of heavy feeling in my tummy. "I don't want to grow up. It doesn't sound like fun at all."

Mom pulls a funny face. "Oh, I dunno. It's not all bad. Sometimes growing up means you can get away from things."

"Grandpa," I say meaningfully.

"He's not as bad as all that," says Mom. "He's just got . . . high standards."

"Nan should tell him to be nicer," I say.

Mom smiles ruefully. "She hates upsetting anyone. She's not the sort of person to stand up to things."

"Auntie Maggi is," I say. Auntie Maggi is Mom's older sister.

"Oh yes, Maggi's always stood up to him," Mom says, but the tone in her voice suggests she disapproves. "Maggie can't back down on anything. It's no wonder she and Dad won't talk to each other anymore." Her eyes dip into the box. "I'm sure they haven't sent me the right number of Gleam 'n' Glow. . . ."

"Are we going to see Auntie Maggi again soon?" I ask hopefully. I'm never quite sure exactly what Auntie Maggi does as her job. It's something to do with PR, which as far as I can tell involves "coming up with ideas" for people, and being paid for it. She told us once about a "campaign" she'd been working on. It seemed to involve lots of phrases like "mental kaleidoscope" and "bringing the outside inside." I listened and it all sounded amazing, and then afterward I realized I hadn't actually understood any of it. I think it was something to do with perfume.

Because she's in PR, Auntie Maggi gets loads of free- bies from events she goes to—"I'm positively drowning in goodie bags, dahling"—and she never seems to want any of them, so I always come home with loads of stuff. That's why I like going to visit! "Mmm," says Mom. "Not sure. She's not in a very good place right now."

"You mean Detroit?"

Mom laughs briefly. "No, in her head. She's a bit depressed." The phone rings and she uncurls herself from the floor. "Well, speak of the devil!" she comments, seeing the number on the screen. "Hello, Mags," she says, answering. "How are you doing?"

Mom likes to walk around while she's on the phone. I watch her talking to Auntie Maggi as she wanders across the living room and back again. Today Mom has peachy-brown eye shadow on her lids. I can see that there are at least three different shades on there. She's lined her eyes with dark brown pencil, and you'd hardly know that she was still sad unless you looked very closely and saw the pinkness under the liner. She's wearing a tight T-shirt with the name of her beauty business scrawled across it in gold. Tight jeans and bare feet. Shiny painted toes. And not a scrap of fat on her anywhere.

I look down at my tummy, bulging over my skirt, and pull myself up straighter. The bulge remains. As does the heaviness from earlier.

Mom puts her hand over the mouthpiece and whispers to me, "I think this is going to be a long one. Can you make me a cup of tea?"

"Yeah, OK," I say, getting up and picking my way through the piles of makeup to the kitchen. I put the kettle on and open the cupboard. There's a pack of cookies, unopened. I make my mom's drink and a cup of tea for myself and deliver her mug to the living room.

"*Thank you*," she mouths at me before saying into the phone, "But didn't the doctor say you shouldn't drink while you're on the medication?"

I take the tea and cookies to my room.

I don't eat *all* of them, of course I don't. Not quite.

Elegance

A line of lipstick
A brush of blush
A drape of damask
A sweep of silk

An alphabet of elegance
   But only if
the letters are the right shape
   to begin with

I think
   the emperor
      was right
Fashion isn't
   the clothes
      it's the
         body inside

And if
    you're not
        the right shape

then it's
    not
        elegance

A few days later, Mom's work colleagues drag her out for the evening to cheer her up. I'm asleep when she gets back, but the sound of the apartment door opening wakes me. I hear her thank Rosie and hand over the babysitting money, and the door closes.

I go into the living room, clutching a teddy and rubbing my eyes. "Oh, sorry, love," Mom says, in the middle of removing her heels. "Did I wake you?"

I shake my head. "Doesn't matter."

"Want a cookie?" she suggests. "Dinner was ages ago." She brings me the packet of cookies. There are only three left in the pack. "Gosh, where did these go?" she remarks.

I sit down with her at the table and slide a cookie out of the packet. "Did you have a good evening?"

She pauses for a moment, and then a smile spreads over her face. "Do you know, I did. It was lovely."

I am surprised. She hasn't smiled like that in days. Since Chris left she's not really smiled properly at all, and I've caught her staring blankly out of the window several times. But tonight she looks different. Sort of softer round the edges.

"We went to the King's Arms," she says. "I was a bit

worried we might bump into . . . you know. Chris. But he wasn't there—and that band was back."

"The ones who played the song about a dog?"

She smiles again. "That's right! And the lead singer . . . well. He asked me out."

My heart sinks. "Oh."

"I know what you're thinking," she says quietly. "And you're probably right. But he . . . he asked, and somehow . . . I couldn't say no."

I bite my lip.

"You wait till you hear him sing," she says. "He's so talented."

"Uh-huh," I say.

ROUNDABOUTS

Round and
round and
round they
spin and
even
though you're
moving
fast you
always
end up
in the
same place

Chapter 11

"Today we're going to be looking at poems and writing some ourselves," says Mr. Lenck. There's an outbreak of groans. "We're building on the work we've been doing on families and communication," he goes on, loading up a poem on the smart board. "I'm going to read you this poem and I want you to think about what the poet is saying and what they're not saying."

It's not a very long poem. It's called "My Mask" and it's all about this person's wonderful life, with lots of friends and a big house and a great job, but the imagery in it is really dark. "Beautiful black curtains hang heavy at my expensive windows, blocking the light" reads one line.

It's totally obvious what the poet is really saying: that you can have loads of *stuff* but still be miserable. The whole class gets it—well, all except Harry who just keeps going on about how he's going to be a professional soccer player when he grows up and he'll totally have black curtains at his mansion windows, along with a theater in the basement and a swimming pool on the roof.

"It's sad," says Verity, "because the poet is trying to be two people. And they can't tell anyone how they really feel. That's why it's called 'My Mask'—because the person is hiding who they really are."

Mr. Lenck nods. "That's exactly it, Verity. And that's what we're going to explore through our own poetry. Because all of us, at some point or other, put on a 'mask': We pretend to be fine or happy about something because we're afraid to show how we really feel."

I sit very still, feeling very cold. This is too close to home. This is me—the poet is me, the things Mr. Lenck is describing, they're me, that's what I do. Not occasionally, but *all the time*. I wear a mask, I laugh things off.

I don't want to do this work. These poems will be

shared—they'll be *read*. They might even go up on the wall. I can't let anyone read my secret thoughts.

With a start, I realize everyone else is reaching for paper and pens. "I don't know what to write," Kayma says to me. "I'm just me. I don't wear a mask."

Sanvi says thoughtfully, "I'm going to write about the time my brother won a competition we both entered. We had to draw posters, and mine was way better than his, but he won a prize and I wasn't even a runner-up. I had to pretend to be really happy for him, because my parents told me to. But inside I was really angry and sad."

"Ugh," says Kayma. "That's exactly the right thing for a poem. Trouble is, I just *tell* people if I'm angry or sad. I'm not good at hiding stuff." She turns to me. "What are you going to write about, Jelly?"

I'm still paralyzed with panic. I don't know what to do. And then something kicks in, and I take a breath and smile wickedly and take Option Two, because it's what I do. "I'm going to write about—" I lower my voice and glance around to make sure Mr. Lenck isn't anywhere nearby "—this kid who's meeting the Queen but she really, really needs to use the toilet, and all the time she's saying posh things to the Queen, she's terrified she's going to wet herself."

Kayma is giggling but Sanvi looks doubtful. "Isn't it supposed to be based on ourselves? I mean, real-life experiences?"

"How d'*you* know I've never met the Queen?" I say, winking.

"Right," says Mr. Lenck, "hopefully you've all got some ideas now—"

"Sure have," I mutter, and Kayma giggles again.

"—so I'd like you to get started, please," Mr. Lenck adds. "I'm looking for really good examples of imagery in your poems, things that give us clues into the poet's real feelings."

It takes me about five minutes to write my poem. It's full of references to dripping taps and waterfalls. It's really clever, even if I do say so myself, and I put down my pen in satisfaction.

"Finished already, Angelica?" asks Mr. Lenck, surprised.

"Yup," I say. "You're going to love it."

"Well, sit tight until the others have finished," he tells me, "and then you can share it."

I spend the next ten minutes flicking a tiny rubber

band at Kayma and making her laugh. Sanvi frowns at me. She's taking this piece of work *very* seriously.

Eventually, just as I'm getting really bored, Mr. Lenck calls for pens down, and it's time for feedback. My hand is first in the air, of course, and Mr. Lenck lets me read it out loud.

I stand up, clearing my throat importantly. "It's called 'My Secret Pain,'" I say in a very serious voice.

"Oh," says Mr. Lenck, "I'll just remind everyone that one of our core values is Respect, and so whatever is shared in this classroom needs to be treated with respect. So no laughing at other people's poems."

"That's right," I say, looking sternly down my nose at my classmates. Then I clear my throat again and begin.

There are a few uncertain smiles at the start, and then as it becomes clear what the character's "secret pain" is, people start grinning and then giggling, and by the last line (where the waterfall flows) everyone is properly laughing.

Except Mr. Lenck, who gives a resigned sigh and says, "It's very clever, Angelica, but it's not exactly what I was looking for."

I squirm in my seat as other people stand and read theirs out. Some of them aren't very good, but everyone else has tried to write a serious, rather than a funny, poem. Verity Hughes's is about her parents' divorce. Her mom was so angry with her dad that she told Verity she didn't want to talk about him ever again. So Verity had lots of conversations with her mom where she had to bite her tongue to avoid mentioning him, which was really hard. Her poem contains lots of references to locked boxes and closed doors, which is clever because it's like all the things she wanted to say had to be locked up so that she didn't upset her mom.

When she finishes reading, there's a small silence, and Avalon, who cries at everything, wipes her eyes. "That's very, very good," says Mr. Lenck. "Well done, Verity."

I press my lips together and stare at the table. I should have written a proper poem. If only Mr. Lenck knew what I had in my poetry book at home! He'd know I can do way better than a stupid poem about needing the toilet. But it's too late now, and anyway . . . now everyone knows Verity's secret. Doesn't she *mind*?

I'm a bit quiet on the way to lunch. Verity is ahead of me in the corridor, and some of the kids from our class are talking to her and giving her hugs and saying how brilliant her poem was and how brave she was to share it.

And I think: If I shared how I feel, my fears and my anger . . . would they call *me* brave?

But I don't think they would—because your parents' divorce is one thing, but being fat is another.

* * *

Is this me?
Is this you?
Is this the best that we can do?
Hiding behind a web of lies
Hoping you don't see what's
in my eyes

Keep my secrets safe inside
Can't let you see how the
laughter hurts me
Make myself a clown for you
So no one knows I'm hurting too

* * *

Chapter 12

Mom goes out on a date with Lennon, the singer. I eat half a tube of Pringles while she's out, because I am restless with anxiety and the Pringles are in the cupboard.

I'm ashamed to say I tried to persuade Mom not to go. "Stay here with *meee*!" I said, doing a little dance. "I'm way more fun!"

She laughed, but she went out anyway. "Maybe she thinks he's Mr. Right," Rosie says, eyes fixed as ever on her phone. "Except there's no such thing. Mom says she married Mr. Right and look how that turned out."

Rosie's mom and dad got divorced and now her mom has a girlfriend who, Rosie says, is very cool and runs a marathon every year. "What if you find Mr. Right, and then he turns into Mr. Wrong, and instead you find *Miss* Right?" Rosie adds.

I go to bed but I can't sleep. I wouldn't admit it to my friends, but I'm still bothered by the poems we did in class, even though it's over a week ago now. I was stupid to write that silly poem. I should have made up something more like Sanvi's. I could have done that. Why didn't I?

Why isn't Mom home yet?

It feels like a whole day has passed by the time she comes home, but according to the clock it's 10:57 when the apartment door clicks open. She's *humming*.

I desperately want to get up and ask her how it went, but somehow I can't. I listen to her humming quietly as she moves around the apartment, and I try to remember the last time she sounded as happy as that. The date must have gone well. But that just means it'll be longer before it all goes wrong.

I pull my pillow around the sides of my head to block out the sound, and I squeeze my eyes shut. A black cloud swirls inside me as I finally fall asleep.

The next morning I'm very tired. I kept having weird dreams about laughing faces, and falling into holes and not being able to get out of them. Mom has to pull the duvet off me before I'll get out of bed. "You're going to be late for school," she says.

"Don't care."

"Get up, Jelly." She changes tack and says in a coaxing voice, "I'll make you pancakes with chocolate chips. . . ."

Oooh. I fall out of bed onto the floor with a *flomp*.

My mom makes very good pancakes. She never uses that premixed stuff, she does it from scratch with eggs and flour and milk and sugar. Yum.

She sings along to the radio while she heats up the batter. I look at her suspiciously. "Are you OK?"

She gives me a warm smile. "I am. I had *such* a nice evening with Lennon."

"Oh," I say. "Um . . . good."

Her phone pings and she reads the message. Her face softens and she *literally* says, "Awww."

"That him?" I say, drizzling a generous amount of syrup over the hot pancakes.

"Yes," she says with a sigh. "He's lovely. So funny and kind and talented. I can't think what he sees in me. I felt like such an idiot yesterday evening. He's had all this life experience, traveling the world—he's been to the Great Barrier Reef!—and I've never been further than France, and that was just the once, and it rained all the time."

"You've had life experience too," I point out, feeling quite cross with Lennon for making my mom feel inferior. "It's just different. But it still counts."

"That's what he said," she replies, her eyes softening again. "He said that people all over the world are just the same. It doesn't matter if you're on an estate or in a jungle tribe, everyone still faces the same worries: whether you've got enough to eat or keep warm, how to make friends, how to be safe. How to be happy with what you've got. He said the happiest people he found in the world were the ones who didn't have a lot of *things* but they had love and friendship and music. And if you have a guitar, it doesn't matter where you are in the world because language is a barrier but music is a gateway."

"Wow," I say, staring at her. "That's . . . um . . ." I don't really know what else to say because this isn't the sort of thing Mom's boyfriends usually talk about.

"Anyway," she says, shaking herself as though suddenly remembering I'm there, "I mustn't go on—you'll be late for school!" Her phone rings and she makes a face at the name on the screen. "Oh *great*, it's Maggi again. . . ." With a sigh she swipes to answer, and then says brightly, "Hi, Mags, how are you doing today?"

I take my plate and mug to the kitchen and go to brush my teeth. I don't like looking at myself in the mirror because I don't like what I see, but this morning I stare into my eyes, trying to figure out what I'm thinking and feeling. It's kind of slippery and topsy-turvy. Like trying to grab a wet fish or catch smoke.

As I leave the apartment I hear Mom say, "But, Maggi, you know that's not true. It's your mind playing tricks on you. No one really thinks that about you." She sounds kind and sympathetic, even though I know she's fed up with hearing Maggi's moans.

It makes me think that even when people are grown-ups they wear masks, like in the poem, and sometimes they don't even know they're doing it.

Chapter 13

Of course in the end, I was bound to meet him. It's about a week later—a week filled with pinging texts and Lennon's songs, which Mom plays obsessively. Annoyingly, I like the songs a lot. I even find myself singing them at random moments during the day, which makes me feel very weird.

Then Mom says casually at breakfast one morning, "Oh, Lennon's going to drop by later, after school. He's got an old record player he wants to lend me."

"An old what?"

"Record player. You know, a turntable. What music used to be played on." She chuckles. "Lennon says anyone who loves music needs to listen to it on vinyl."

"Oh," I say. "I . . . OK." What if I come home and they're in the bedroom, like with Chris? "I might go to Coffeetastic after school."

"No, don't," Mom says quickly. "Come and meet him. You'll like him, I know you will. He's different from the others."

At break time, Sanvi says to me, "You OK, Jelly?"

"Me? Yeah—why?"

"You're really quiet. Is something the matter?"

"No," I say, too quickly. "No, I'm fine. Honest." I beam at her, the effort making my cheeks ache.

"Oh," she says. "OK. That's good then. Kayma and I are going to practice our song. Want to come?"

I've heard them sing their song for The K Factor about sixteen times already. "Um . . ." I say, looking around for an escape. I spot it in the form of a bunch of boys heading to the field with a soccer ball. "Sorry, I promised Will Matsunaga I'd teach him how to take a penalty kick. You know how it is." I shrug. "When you're a top soccer player like me . . ."

Sanvi smiles. "It must be hard when you earn so many millions and have to pose for all those photos."

"It *is*," I groan theatrically. "And I daren't pull a muscle, or my career will be *over*."

Sanvi laughs and gives me a wave. "All right. See you in a bit."

Having said I'm going to play soccer, I now have to, in case Kayma and Sanvi find out I was fibbing. I jog over to the field, feeling irritated and stormy.

A game is underway, though it's not clear who's on which team. I run straight into the middle.

"Hey, what are you doing?" Marshall shouts at me. "Get out of the way, Jelly."

"Got a new game for you," I call. Then I stand up straight and tuck my arms into my sides. "It's called Hit the Lamppost. You kick the ball at me. If you hit me, you get one point. I'm a wide-enough target—it should be easy!"

The boys look at each other and laugh. "You're crazy, Jelly," Will says.

"Go on then," says one of the other boys.

I place myself in the middle of the goal, standing up straight. "From the penalty spot!" I tell them. "No closer!"

The boys line up to take turns kicking the ball at me.

Most of them miss. Will is good, he hits me twice.

The ball bounces off me, leaving a stinging pain. But in some weird way the pain is good. It's easier to deal with than the big swirling worry in my stomach, and it means I don't have to think about meeting Lennon after school. And the boys are all laughing and having a brilliant time, and when the bell rings they rush over to slap me on the back and tell me I'm a good sport—and I feel *good*. So making myself a figure of fun was worth it.

I drag my feet on the way home. The sun is shining, but there's still a dark stormy cloud inside me because I can't put it off any longer. I'd like to fast-forward to tomorrow.

As I go through the park, I hear a vaguely familiar sound. A tinny melody. I look around to see where it's coming from. A man is sitting on one of the benches, holding something small to his mouth. Of course—it's a harmonica. The instrument the man in Coffeetastic showed me. For a moment I feel a clutch of hope that it's the same man, but it isn't. The man on the bench is older, with a bald patch on the top of his head and graying tufts around it. Despite the hot weather he's wearing a sort of brown woollen suit, with a pale blue shirt and battered Converses. In a weird retro way, he looks kind of stylish.

The tune he's playing is lilting and mournful. I stand and listen for a few moments, but then I realize it might look weird if he sees me standing there staring at him, so I move on. The haunting tune follows me out of the park, like a lost dog.

I feel calmer by the time I reach home. It's almost as though the tune was saying to me: It's all right. You can do this. You just have to be the Jelly everyone knows, and not let things get to you. Whoever this new boyfriend is, he won't be around for long. Smile and nod, and keep out of the way.

I'll say hi and go to my room and maybe look up harmonica videos online.

And then I open the door and nearly fall over in shock. Because standing at the dining table, chatting animatedly to my mom as he puts a black disc onto an ancient record player, is the man from Coffeetastic.

Chapter 14

"You!" I say, astonished.

"You!" he says back, equally surprised, it seems. Then a smile spreads across his face, and it's wide and warm and his eyes sparkle, and he adds, "Well, hello again!"

Mom looks baffled. "You two have already met?"

He lets out a laugh of genuine amusement. "Oh, this is so great! I had no idea! You're Angelica then?"

"Jelly," I say automatically. "Everyone calls me Jelly."

"All right," he replies, nodding. "Jelly it is. I'm Lennon."

"You're Lennon." I must have realized this when I

walked in, but my brain is only just catching up with my eyes. "I can't believe it."

Lennon says to Mom, "I met Jelly in a coffee shop a couple of weeks ago. She was kind enough to share her table."

Mom frowns. "When were you in a coffee shop without me?"

Uh-oh. "Um . . ."

"You were on your way home from school, weren't you?" Lennon breaks in. "You didn't stay long."

"Er—yeah, that's right," I say, throwing him a grateful look. "I just popped in to say hi to Fliss, that's all. And have a drink."

"You shouldn't let a stranger share your table," Mom tells me, changing tack. "It's not safe."

"It was very busy," Lennon says. "Hers was the only table with a spare chair. We were very sensible about it, weren't we, Jelly?"

I nod. "We talked about music."

"Hmm," says Mom.

"Speaking of," Lennon says, "want to see some ancient music technology? I'm educating your mom."

Lennon shows me the record player which is in a case,

kind of like a really big laptop. The lid lifts up to reveal a round platform with a metal peg in the middle and a wobbly arm on the side. At the end of the arm, a sharp needle points downward. "This is a record," Lennon says, holding up a black disc as big as our dinner plates, with a small hole in the middle. "Or an LP. Made of vinyl. See the grooves on it? That's where the music is stored."

"I *have* seen one of these before," I say witheringly. "Kayma's dad has one. They're totally retro."

He laughs. "Yeah, they must seem historic to you. Like the wireless was to me."

I don't follow this. "Wireless?"

"Never mind." Lennon slots the disc onto the platform, lifts the metal arm, and carefully lines it up on the edge of the disc. Then he flicks a switch, and the record starts going round—and music comes out.

It's a band playing some kind of old-fashioned music. I saw a black-and-white program once about people in America on paddle steamers and cutting sugar. Something like that anyway. There was music like this playing on the soundtrack. Then a familiar tinny sound picks out a mournful melody. "Harmonica!" I exclaim.

"That's right." Lennon grins at me. "Did you listen to some Stevie Wonder then?"

"No. No, I meant to, but I forgot."

"You two seem to have had quite a lot of conversation in the coffee shop," says Mom, and her voice sounds a bit odd.

"I'll bring some Stevie Wonder next time," Lennon says. Then he turns to Mom and adds, "If that's all right with you, of course."

"Of course it is," she says with a bright smile.

I watch the record going around and around, and the needle in the player skimming the grooves. It's kind of hypnotic. The song sounds different from what I'm used to, not just because it's old and jazzy, but sort of raw and immediate. Like the singer is right here in the room with us, voice cracking on a note and everything. If I close my eyes, I can imagine the band here in our living room, the bass drum pedal thumping on our carpet, and the musicians breathing. There are little scrapes and rustles in the music, as though the air is alive with it. Briefly I imagine I have a music net that I can sweep through the air to capture the fluttering sounds.

When the song ends, Lennon switches off the player and lifts the metal arm with the needle off the record.

"What did you think?" he asks.

"Was that their final version?" I ask. "Only, it sounded kind of like a rehearsal."

Lennon laughs. "That's the immediacy of the recording. You don't get any of the polish from computer processing."

"The singer was a bit out of tune at one point," I say, "but I liked how he put lots of feeling into it."

"Do you sing, Jelly?" Lennon asks.

"Oh, no, not really. I mean, I *can*. But it's not my thing."

"She has a beautiful voice," Mom breaks in. She pulls me to her and puts her arms around me tightly. "It's probably because she's built like an opera singer. Big and solid and strong, my Jelly."

The words sting, and her arms are too tight. "Yeah," I say, and grin at Lennon. "It's not over till the fat lady sings, Mom always says. So beware the day I sing!"

He laughs because I'm smiling, and then he says lightly, "Don't be silly—you're not fat."

A chill runs down my spine, but I don't need to reply because Mom lets go of me and leans over the record player. "I've never really listened to one of these," she says. "It's so vivid, so fresh. I mean, it sounds old, but like it's still alive. Like history is talking to you, or something."

Lennon says enthusiastically, "That's exactly how it makes me feel. Shall we try another track?"

We sit down and listen to some more songs on the record, and Lennon talks about how he first got interested in music as a boy, when his dad bought him a guitar. "It was way too big for me," he says, smiling. "My hand wouldn't go round the fretboard and I could only play three chords. But three chords can be all you need for a song. I guess that's how I got into jazz and blues, because loads of those songs are just built on easy repetition of a couple of chords. Basic twelve-bar blues only needs three chords. I could teach both of you in an afternoon. And once you've got the basics you can sing all kinds of stuff. I used to make up little songs about how I hated going to school. How the PE teacher was a sadist, making us run round the field in pouring rain. There was even a song I wrote called 'English Hell,' because I was dyslexic and always came in last."

I laugh, but Mom says, "Oh, poor you."

"Don't worry, it was funny. The song, I mean. '*The sun is gone, now rings the bell, that summons me to English hell.*' I was pleased with that rhyme."

"Sounds like you used music as your way to cope with the world," says Mom, leaning on her hand and gazing at him.

"Yeah, I guess I did. Life wasn't all that much fun, you know? But I always had my music."

Later, when Lennon has gone and Mom and I are eating baked potatoes, she says to me, "Isn't he nice? I told you you'd like him."

I add another handful of grated cheese to my potato. I feel a bit weird. Lennon *is* nice—so nice, in fact, that it makes me feel unsettled. He's so different from anyone else Mom has gone out with. He's interesting and talks about himself in an interesting way. Chris used to talk about himself too, but it would always be about how much money he was saving for a new car, or how some insurance firm tried to scam him, or how some idiot stole his parking space at work. Lennon talks about learning things, and being unhappy, and finding something you love to do. I don't think I've ever heard a man talk about those things before. Not unless you count Mr. Collery in second grade, who was really good at sorting out friendship problems and bullying because he actually listened and was sympathetic, and told us about his own experiences of being bullied at school.

But Mom doesn't usually go out with people like Mr. Collery. And when Lennon was talking about using music as a way to express stuff he couldn't tell people . . . it made me think of my pink poetry book under my pillow, hiding all my secrets.

Mom sighs happily. "I don't want to jinx things . . . but I really think he's something special."

I glance at her. "Did you really like his music? The record player and everything?"

"Of course I did. Well—" she digs at her cheese-less potato "—I wasn't sure to start with. It takes a bit of getting used to. It's not the kind of music I normally listen to. But that's good, isn't it? I mean, trying something new? And I wouldn't want to upset him when he'd brought it over specially."

So she pretended. Another mask. Like me pretending to find something funny when it isn't.

Is everyone pretending? I wonder.

How do you know
        when something's real?
How do you know
        just what to feel?
How can you tell
        if something's true?
How can you tell
        the real you?
How can you be
        an honest friend?
How can you know
        when to pretend?
What if it's all
        a point of view?
What if we're all
        just stumbling through?

Chapter 15

To my disappointment, Lennon doesn't come around again for a few days. But he has lent me his harmonica, and I listen to lots of Stevie Wonder and Sonny Boy Williamson, and then I come across a man and a woman who do harmonica duets of pop songs, and I watch them for hours.

Playing the harmonica isn't as easy as it looks. In the first lesson I find online, the man explains how to play a single note. The clever thing about harmonicas is that when you breathe out it plays one note, and when you breathe in it plays a different note. *In the same place!* Two notes from the same hole. But it's hard to play just one note at a time because the holes are close together, and other notes leak into your mouth.

Mom's not impressed. "Do you have to play the same thing over and over?" she says, rolling her eyes.

"It's called practicing," I say. "I can't get good at it if I don't practice, can I?"

"Yeah, but how long before you can play a tune?" She's just received another delivery and is busy unpacking it all. "They've left off my Gleam 'n' Glow *again*! Louise is going to kill me. She's been waiting for six weeks now." She taps a message into her phone and sends it. "I'm going to find out if the other agents have got theirs. I'm beginning to think someone at the warehouse doesn't like me."

She starts digging around in the box again, so I try another run of notes on the harmonica.

"Oh, Jelly, for goodness sake!" she suddenly snaps. "Can't you go and make that awful noise in your bedroom? I'm trying to concentrate."

Wow, she is in a bad mood today. I'm almost at the door when she suddenly says, in a pretend-casual voice, "Oh, by the way, Nan and Grandpa are coming over this evening."

Ah. No wonder she's in a mood. "What time?" I ask, trying to pretend I don't mind.

"Six. So . . . I dunno, tidy your bedroom or something."

My bedroom is clean already. "OK," I say. I go to my room and put the harmonica away. I don't feel like playing now.

By the time they arrive, Mom has cleared all the packaging from the living room and vacuumed it, plumped the sofa cushions ("Don't sit on them, you'll squash them!"), straightened out the coffee table, and lit a scented candle.

The first thing Grandpa says when he comes in is, "What's that godawful smell?"

Grandpa isn't a tall man. He's wide and stocky, with feet that turn out a bit like a penguin's. He's not fat but somehow takes up a lot of room. When he sits down, he spreads his legs apart, which Mom calls "manspreading" and it's true I've never seen a woman sit like that. Grandpa's eyes are gray-blue, and they're almost always annoyed.

Today he gives Mom a brief hug and then holds her by the shoulders, looking her up and down. "You all right?"

he says. "You look tired. Hope you're not burning the candle at both ends, especially if they all smell as bad as this one!" He bursts into raucous laughter and his eyes slide across to me. "How are you, Jelly? Growing fast, aren't you? What are you *feeding* this girl, Arlene? She on steroids or something?" He laughs again.

I feel myself shrivel inside.

"Dad . . ." says Mom weakly. "Jelly is *fine*."

"Of course she is," says Nan, who as usual has faded into the background. Now she comes forward and gives me a hug. She feels light and fragile, like a bird, and she smells of talcum powder and worry. "She's perfect, aren't you?"

I smile back at her, but no one takes any notice of what Nan says because Grandpa doesn't listen to her, so she never gets her voice heard.

Grandpa sits down on the sofa, taking up almost all of it. "I see you still haven't mended that shelf, Arlene," he says, his gaze fastening on a gap on the wall that's been there for a while, ever since a shelf gave way. "Can't your man fix it? That Chris guy?"

"I'm not seeing Chris anymore," Mom says, and clears her throat.

Grandpa makes a *pfft* sound and shakes his head. "Let

another one slip through your fingers, did you?"

"He wasn't very nice," I blurt out, because Mom looks stricken. "He didn't treat Mom well."

Mom glances at me, but her eyes are hard, not grateful.

"It takes two to tango," says Grandpa, which makes no sense to me at all.

"I've got to sort dinner," Mom says, turning away.

Nan jumps up. "I'll help, love." She trots out after her.

I do *not* want to be left in the room with Grandpa. But as I follow the others, Mom turns and says in a low voice, "Jelly, keep your grandpa company."

I bite my lip. "Umm . . ."

"Why not tell Grandpa what sports you've been playing at school?" Nan suggests, reaching out to smooth my hair back from my face. "You know he loves sports."

I heave a sigh. I do know Grandpa loves sports. Watching, that is, not playing them. He'll watch almost any sport because he loves to complain about referees and umpires. "All right," I say, and drag my feet back into the living room. *Respect your elders,* Mom says. *He's the only grandpa you've got.* So I force my mouth into a smile.

"Am I going to be offered a drink?" Grandpa says mildly as I approach. He's leaning forward and examining the DVD shelf. "What a load of nonsense your mother watches."

"Would you like a drink?" I ask.

"Glass of wine, thanks." His eyes are still on the shelf. "What kind of romantic rubbish is this?" He plucks out a DVD with two smiling couples on the front. It's *The Holiday*, a film Mom's watched about fifty gazillion times.

"Grandpa would like a glass of wine," I call to the kitchen.

"What color?" Mom shouts back.

"What color?" I ask Grandpa.

He shrugs. "Whatever."

"He doesn't care!" I relay to the kitchen.

Honestly, you'd think our apartment was huge.

I don't really know what to say to him, but Grandpa is still looking at *The Holiday*. He taps the picture of the blonde woman. "She's not so bad. Look at her big smile!" He sits back, dropping the DVD onto the coffee table and spreading his legs again. "Young women are too serious these days. All of this feminism stuff—what happened to just having a good time?"

I don't really understand what Grandpa is talking about. My mom runs her own business, and when she goes out with her friends, she has a good time. I'm not sure if that makes her a feminist or not.

Nan suggested I talk about sports so I clutch at the first thought that comes into my head. "When I go to Marston Junior High, I'll be learning rugby." Rugby is one of Grandpa's favorite sports.

He stares at me. "What? Marston what?"

"My new school," I say. "In September. They do rugby in the autumn."

"They teach *girls* rugby?" he says. "For the love of Pete, why?"

Oh, brother. Wrong thing to say.

"Rugby's a man's game," Grandpa starts up. "Girls don't need to run off aggression like the boys do." He gives a bark of laughter. "No point teaching girls rugby—they'll be far too worried about breaking their nails or getting muddy!" Then he starts going on about how girls should play "safe" things like basketball, which has no contact, and tennis, because they look good in short skirts, and I close my ears, nod along, and start composing a poem in my head.

I AM GIRL

I am MUD
I am BLOOD
I am MAKEUP
I can BREAKUP
I am DREAMS — I am SCHEMES
I am HATE — I am GREAT
I am STRONG
I BELONG
I can FIGHT
I have MIGHT

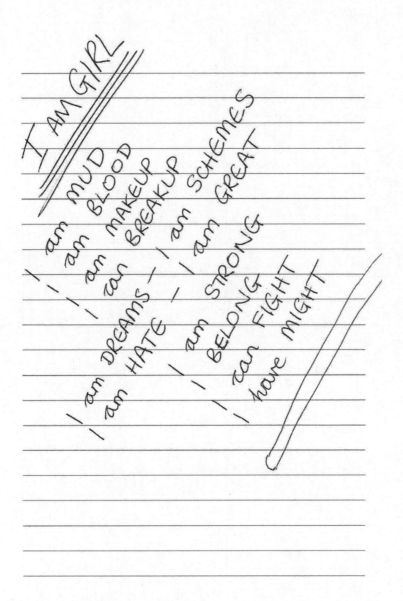

I'm a WHIRL
I AM GIRL
you ignore?
HEAR ME ROAR

Chapter 16

Grandpa has another glass of wine with his dinner, which is overcooked because Mom left the meat in for too long. She's always nervous when they're here. Grandpa helpfully points this out. "If you want a husband," he tells her, "you'll have to improve your cooking."

I think Grandpa is perhaps a time traveler. He must have come from about a hundred years ago to say things like that. Sanvi's dad runs a restaurant and he's an amazing cook. Sanvi says her mom is nowhere near as good as her dad at making curry and chapatis.

"Maybe Mom doesn't want a husband," I say

cheerfully, trying without much success to cut through my slice of beef.

"Jelly . . ." says Mom, in a kind of hopeless, please-don't way.

"Of course she wants a husband," Grandpa says. "She's always wanted to get married, ever since she was a little girl." He grins. "Used to spend hours designing her wedding dress, choosing her bridesmaids—remember how they were always changing, depending on who her friends were?" He suddenly addresses Nan, who flinches slightly in surprise.

She smiles. "Oh, yes. Sometimes it was Jessica and Ruby. Other times she'd have fallen out with them and it'd be Vicki or Candice."

"Candice?" Grandpa says. "Oh, yes—the black girl. Didn't her father go to prison? Typical."

I chew my beef fiercely. Grandpa looks down on practically everyone. Trying to point it out is like trying to drain a lake by standing in it and using a bucket. It's too big, you don't know where to start, and you know you'll never make a difference. Plus it's likely to drown you.

I can see why Auntie Maggi argued a lot with him. Auntie Maggi believes in things like homeopathy and libraries, saving old trees, and helping the homeless. Grandpa thinks anything herbal is "New Age trash" and that the homeless "should get jobs like the rest of us." It's quite hard to like Grandpa, but Mom keeps trying, so I do too.

After dinner Grandpa switches on the TV without asking and finds a sports channel, though he grumbles that we don't have the ones he likes. "I'll have a cup of tea while you're making one," he calls.

No one was making a cup of tea, but now they are.

I help Mom and Nan in the kitchen, washing and drying and putting things away.

"How are things with you, Jelly?" Nan asks, passing me a saucepan to dry. "It must feel strange, being in your last year of elementary school. Do you feel ever so big?" Then she gives a little gasp and gets horribly flustered. "I mean, big because you're one of the oldest in the school, not big because . . . You're not *big*, you're beautiful, never let anyone tell you different. Oh, dear."

"It's all right," I tell her, though inside I am sighing. "I know what you meant. Yeah, I do feel old. Everyone looks so little. It's cool being in the top year at school though."

Nan is still flushed and flustered. She shoots me a

trembling smile. "Are you looking forward to moving on? Will your friends be going to the same school with you?"

"Yes," I say. "Kayma and Sanvi are coming to Marston Junior High too. It's way bigger though; I don't know if we'll be in the same classes."

"I'm sure you'll make lots of new friends," Nan says. "You're such a bubbly sort of person—it's a great asset." She pats me on the shoulder. "People like confidence, they'll be drawn to you."

I smile back. Nan has no idea all my confidence is pretend.

"I think you can take up a new instrument in your first year," Mom says. "I'm sure I read it somewhere."

My jaw drops. "Really? *Really* really?"

She laughs. "It's about time you learned an instrument."

"The harmonica is an instrument," I say.

"Harmonica?" Nan asks. "What made you pick that up then?"

"Oh," I say, "it's because—"

Mom interrupts, "Oh, you know how she gets these obsessions over things, Mom. Harmonica is the latest. She's watching all these videos and teaching herself."

I close my mouth. Mom doesn't want me to mention Lennon, that's clear. So I smile at Nan and say, "When I've learned how to play properly, I'll play you a tune."

"That would be lovely," Nan says. "Maybe your mom can sing along. Always did have such a nice voice. I remember her singing in the school nativity. Angelic, she was."

"Dad said I couldn't hold a tune in a bucket," Mom comments.

"Oh, you mustn't take that kind of thing seriously," Nan says. "He likes his little jokes. And everyone agreed you looked beautiful in that white dress, with tinsel in your hair. The other moms said I should sign you up as a child model."

"Why didn't you?" I ask.

"Grandpa wouldn't have it." Nan glances into the living room and lowers her voice. Not that she needs to. Grandpa is glued to a Formula One race, and the noise from the zooming cars would drown out anything we were saying. "Said modeling wasn't decent. He doesn't approve of anything like that. Fashion, the beauty business . . ."

There's a tiny pause. Mom's lips have gone very thin.

Nan's eyes widen in dismay. "Oh, sweetheart, I didn't

mean *you*. We're very proud of you for running your own business, you know we are. We just want you to be happy."

Mom says nothing.

Nan glances into the living room again and sighs. "Grandpa doesn't mean to upset anyone. He just is who he is, you know?"

There doesn't seem to be much anyone can say to that.

Back in the day there were
record players and
two-mile walks to school and
winters so cold they bit at your
knees.
Coal on the fire and
bread and gravy and
Solitaire with marbles.
Boys played rugby
Girls learned to type
Black people knew their place
Which was anywhere but here
And you could be friends but
they weren't People Like You.
Now there are
smartphones and
social networks and
I'm Lovin' It and
Xbox games
Girl football is on TV
Men can marry men

and you can be friends with
whoever you flipping like
Except
there are still people like
my grandad, who
don't realize
it's no longer
back in the day.

Chapter 17

The next time Lennon comes around, I am practically bursting with excitement. I've taught myself a tune on the harmonica, and I'm so nervous, it's slippery under my hands and I have to play it three times before I get it right.

He beams at me. "Brilliant! I know it too—it's by the Hollies. One of my favorite songs. Great job. You must have been practicing loads!"

"All the time," Mom murmurs, but she says it nicely. She went a bit shy when Lennon arrived. She even blushed!

"Hey, can I play along?" Lennon asks. He gestures toward his guitar bag by the door.

A thrill runs through me. "Um . . . I guess."

He gets out the guitar and starts tuning it, picking at a string to make sure it matches a note on another string. Then he strums a couple of chords and looks up at me. The guitar nestles in his lap like a well-behaved pet. "Shall I count us in?" he asks.

"OK."

"Two, three, four . . ."

I don't play it very well, but it sort of doesn't matter, because Lennon strums gently along underneath my tune, waiting when I take a little too long to find the next note, and not trying to go too fast or anything. It makes me feel . . . well, I'm not sure. Like there's something inside me that I didn't know was there.

When I finish, I have to swallow because I have this weird feeling like I need to cry.

Mom says quietly, "Aww. That was lovely." Her eyes are all shiny as she looks between me and Lennon.

Lennon smiles and says, "Shall we do the whole song? The harmonica solo comes in the middle. I'll tell you when to come in."

And then, sitting right there on our sofa, in the very

spot where Grandpa sat and spouted his venom, Lennon sings this beautiful song about love and brothers and long roads, and Mom and I sit spellbound and watch his fingers dance across the fretboard. When Lennon says, "Ready for your solo, Jelly?" I drop the harmonica in my haste, because I've forgotten I needed to play. But he waits for me to start, as though it's no bother at all, and I play it much better this time, and then he finishes the song, and Mom sniffs and says, "I need a tissue," and runs off to the bathroom.

Lennon smiles at me. "What do you think?"

I don't say anything right away, which is unusual for me. "It feels like . . . ice and honey," I say. "Sweet and chilly at the same time."

His smile widens so far it sets diamonds sparkling in his eyes. "A perfect way to describe it. You're quite a poet, young lady."

I hesitate. "I do write poems actually."

"You do? That's great. Your mom never said."

"She doesn't know," I say, my eyes flicking quickly to the bathroom. "Don't tell her—"

Mom comes back in, and I feel panicky. But Lennon begins to strum something new, and he gives me a gentle nod before he says, "Want to hear one of mine this time?" and I know he'll keep my secret.

Mom curls up in the armchair and watches Lennon as he sings a song about a girl who doesn't know he's there. Her eyes are soft and her whole body looks different. It takes me a moment to realize she looks relaxed. Mom's usually on the go: Even when she's sitting drinking green tea and talking to me, her body is tense, as though ready for the next thing. Right now though she looks . . . still. Calm. And the expression on her face . . . I'm not sure I've seen it before. The tiny lines around her eyes have disappeared.

I look back at Lennon. His eyes are closed as he sings, and the muscles in his arm flex as he changes chords. He exists in his own world, I think he's even forgotten we're here. In his world, he's completely *him*. We can only watch from the outside.

When he opens his eyes, it's not at me he looks but at Mom, and it's almost like there's a kind of silent fizz when their eyes meet, like electricity.

I don't really want to go, but I feel I ought to, because there's something private happening that I'm not part of. So I get up and go to my bedroom while they're still looking at each other.

Eyes meet
across the room
Meet and stick
Glued to a tune
of beating hearts
in harmony
laid out for all
the world to see
Ice and honey
Cold and sweet
Love and eyes
and music meet

Chapter 18

A couple of days later, Mom says, "Lennon suggested we have a picnic on Saturday."

I'm surprised. Picnics aren't a thing we do normally. "Where?"

"I don't know exactly. Lennon's picking us up and driving us into the country."

The country sounds exotic. We don't leave the city much. "Will he bring his guitar?"

Mom laughs. "I expect so. He never goes anywhere without it."

It's not until later in the day I realize what was odd

about the conversation. Mom's laugh sounded different. Like a real one.

Saturday is a sunny day, and Mom spends ages getting ready. "This top?" she asks me repeatedly. "Or this one? I don't want to get too warm. But on the other hand, Lennon said he liked the blue one when I wore it. Or should I ditch them and go for the gray dress?" She looks in the mirror and turns sideways, placing a hand on her tummy. "No, I can't wear that. Look how my stomach sticks out!"

Her stomach does not stick out. No more than a stomach is supposed to—after all, there are major organs in there.

"What are *you* wearing?" she suddenly demands, switching her attention to me.

I glance down. "This?" I'm in purple leggings and a cream T-shirt with a glittery flower on it. The T-shirt says, "Pretty as a flower" in swirly writing. Mom bought it for me.

She frowns a bit. "I suppose it'll do. Should I wear leggings too then? I don't want to overdress. But I want to look nice."

"You look nice in anything," I offer. As soon as

I've said it, I bite my lip because she hates it when I compliment her. I brace myself, expecting her to tell me off.

But instead, she reaches out to cup my chin with her hand, and her eyes soften as she says, "What a kind thing to say. Thank you, darling."

I am filled with warmth. I don't think I've *ever* heard my mom accept a compliment. I throw my arms around her. "You're so beautiful," I say. "You could wear a trash bag and still be the most beautiful mom ever."

Her arms tighten around me. "Ah, sweetheart," she says.

There's a *ping* and I look down at her phone on the dressing table next to me. It says: "Message from Chris." Mom reaches out and deletes the message without reading it. Then she goes back to her clothes dilemma.

I smile.

By the time Lennon arrives, Mom has finally chosen an outfit and done her makeup accordingly. I've had a second breakfast.

Lennon grins at me when I open the door. "You okay, Jelly?" He's wearing a white shirt that reminds me of a pirate, with his usual brown jacket and jeans.

"Did you bring your guitar?" I ask.

"It's in the car. You going to bring the harmonica?"

"Yes!" I run to my room.

He calls after me, "We're going to need to find your mom a musical instrument to play." Then I hear her say behind me in a soft voice, "I already have one, don't I?" and he chuckles and I can tell they're kissing, and even though I like him, that whole thing is still *ugh*, so I take longer than I need to find the harmonica.

Lennon's car is eight years old and a VW Golf. Inside, the seats are covered in crumbs and there are a couple of discarded wrappers under the seat that I decide not to mention. He has an air freshener in the shape of cherries hanging from the rearview mirror. The car does not smell of cherries.

We drive out of town and Lennon plays some gospel music on the way. It's lots of people singing, sometimes about God, and they sound pretty happy. "We used to sing this one in my school choir," Mom comments suddenly.

Lennon turns to look at her. "Hey, I should get you to sing with me."

Mom goes all red and flustered. "Oh no, I don't do

that kind of thing. My voice isn't very good."

"I bet you're better than you think," he says.

"I'd much rather listen to *you* singing," Mom says, putting a hand on Lennon's knee. He smiles, and then says, "Here we are."

"Here" is a narrow street, in a village, with houses on each side. "Where's the country?" I ask.

Lennon laughs. "Hiding. Don't worry, we'll find it. We're going on an adventure."

Adventure. I like the sound of that.

In the trunk of the car is a large backpack. I'm slightly disappointed it isn't a basket. Aren't picnics supposed to be with baskets? I read a book once about a bunch of kids who went on a picnic, and they definitely had a basket. But I suppose a backpack is more practical. Lennon hefts it onto his back and then picks up his guitar. He grins at me. "Ready?"

"Yeah."

He holds out his spare hand to my mom, who takes it. "This way."

The houses on this street all look like they're slightly squashed. The roofs aren't straight, and the windows are a bit wonky. They look very old. In fact, one of them has a little plaque above the front door with the date 1743 on it. "Wow," I say. Our block of apartments is only fifty years old. This house is ancient.

"I grew up in a house like that," Lennon says. "They're all good and well, but you do get a lot of spiders."

Mom shudders. "Yuck. I can't stand spiders."

This is true. Whenever there's a spider in the apartment, it's me who has to hit it with a magazine. I know I should catch it in a glass and put it outside, but I can't. I'm brave but not *that* brave.

Between two houses is a gap with a wooden stile. A wooden post stands next to it with a "Footpath" arrow at the top. "Off we go," says Lennon.

On the other side of the stile is a narrow shady path. The hedges on either side are tall and thick. The path is stony and studded with weeds, and I step around the occasional nettle sticking out from the hedge. "I'm totally wearing the wrong thing," Mom moans. She went for a long skirt in the end, with ballet flats. They are definitely the wrong thing, though I didn't think of that when she was asking my opinion. I'm glad I'm wearing sneakers.

I like the strange narrow green corridor. It feels like there could be something exciting at the end of it.

Lennon is leading, and he steps back when he reaches

the end of the path because there's a clever swinging gate. "Kissing gate," he says.

I wrinkle my nose. "Ew."

He laughs as he goes through it. "Yeah, I guess it is a bit. I remember being your age and thinking everything like that was 'ew.' While secretly hoping one day I'd be able to kiss someone."

My face goes red. "Shuddup . . ."

"Jelly's a superstar," Mom says, coming through the gate behind me. "She's got such a big personality, she'll have her pick of boyfriends."

Big personality. Big personality to go with her big body. I shake off the sudden prickle of shame between my shoulder blades.

"Or girlfriends," Lennon adds.

Mom raises her eyebrows. "Or girlfriends. Who knows?"

Beyond the kissing gate, the path opens out onto a field. Suddenly the sky is twice as big. I can see one house, far off in the distance, but otherwise there's just field and hedges and sky. And . . .

"Horses!" I cry. Our footpath continues along the side of the field, but to our left a fence has been created out of posts and tape, and on the other side are three horses:

one brown, one black, and one white. They are grazing on the grass a little ways off. I call to them. "Hello! Here! Come and say hello!" and make that clicking noise with my tongue that people always make to horses.

The horses look up but only one saunters over: the black one. "He's hoping you have some treats," Mom says. "It's a shame we didn't bring any carrots."

"Aha!" says Lennon, and swings the backpack onto the ground. Then he starts rummaging through it.

"Did you bring carrots?" I ask him, reaching over the taped fence to try and touch the soft velvety nose of the black horse. I suppose it might be a pony, not a horse. There's a difference, though I can't remember what.

"No . . ." says Lennon, digging around in the bag. "But I did bring apples. Here you go."

I hold it out to the horse on a flat hand. He whiffles his nose and then reaches out. My hand is covered in slobbery horse lick as he munches the apple from it. It tickles and makes me laugh.

"Oh, Jelly," says Mom. "Your hand—that's disgusting."

I stroke the horse's nose. "It doesn't matter. Horses are really big, aren't they? I mean, when you see them on television or something, they don't look as big as they really are. How would you get on this one? Its back is higher than my head!"

"I always wanted riding lessons," Mom says. "Maggi and I begged for them, but Dad said they cost too much and there wasn't much point unless you were going to be a champion jockey or something, and girls didn't do that kind of thing, so . . ." She gives a rueful smile. "Maggi wouldn't speak to him for a whole week after that."

"Well, maybe for your next birthday I'll buy you a riding lesson," Lennon says. "Because that sucks."

Mom smiles, and I can see sunlight reflected in her eyes.

"Grandpa's like that," I say to Lennon. "He doesn't want anyone to have any fun. Especially girls. He thinks girls aren't as good as boys."

Mom tells me off. "It's not that, Jelly. He's just from a different time, that's all."

"What—the eighteenth century?" I retort. "Mr. Lenck is practically the same age, and *he* doesn't think like that." I turn to Lennon. "You don't think boys are better than girls, do you?"

He hesitates, and the breath catches in my throat. I've never asked a man that question, certainly not one of Mom's boyfriends. I'm suddenly afraid of the answer.

"I don't think that, no," Lennon says slowly. He frowns at the horse. "But I think there are some things boys do better than girls, and some things girls do better than boys."

I fold my arms. "Like what?"

"Jelly . . ." Mom sounds embarrassed. "Don't spoil things."

"No, no, it's a good question," Lennon says. "I don't mind answering it. Hang on, let me just get my thoughts in order." He stares at the ground for a moment and then says, "I think, for example, that girls are better at owning up when they feel sad. They're good at asking their friends for help. But boys are better at switching off from worry stuff. You know, when we're watching the soccer game or playing music, or . . . I dunno, going for a run, we're not thinking about a million things at once. Girls and women have too much going on in their brains that they don't seem to be able to switch off." He pauses. "Well, the women *I* know, that is. I mean, not everyone is the same. I do have a friend—a guy—who worries about stuff all the time. But then he struggles with anxiety, so he finds it harder to get his thoughts under control."

I stare at him. "Are you *sure* you're a man?" I ask suspiciously.

He bursts out laughing.

"It's only," I say, "that I've never heard a man say stuff like that before."

"No?" He smiles at me. "Well, maybe that's because men aren't very good at saying this kind of thing. There you go, another thing that girls do better."

I turn to Mom. "Do you feel like you have too much going on in your brain?"

She is gazing at Lennon and her eyes are soft and wet. "All the time," she says, before turning away and saying in a completely different tone, "Are we going to eat this picnic anytime soon?"

There's a red bus goes down our road
every day, same time 9:47
The same people stand at the bus stop
waiting for the red bus.
One day I was waiting with them
and the bus came.
We all got on.
I sat with Mom upstairs.
Behind me I heard a man talk
        about the red bus.
I turned around to say,
        "it's blue"
"No, it isn't," he said back
"The bus is red.
It's always been red.
The 9:47 bus is red.
You just didn't look properly."

I sat in my seat,
my face red
from being corrected.

When we got off the bus
I turned to look.

The bus was blue.
That day the red bus was blue.

I looked for the man but he had gone
So I couldn't have my moment of triumph.
And when I told my mom
She said,
"Does it really matter?"
But it did
Because the man hadn't seen
what he thought he'd seen.

It just shows
You don't always know
what you think you know.

Chapter 19

We find a bench overlooking a dip in the fields for our picnic. Lennon says it's not a proper picnic if you don't sit on the ground though, and he unrolls a picnic blanket—one of those ones with fabric on the top and a waterproof layer underneath. Even Mom sits on the blanket, and we use the bench as a table.

Lennon says apologetically, "I didn't know what you both liked to eat, so I brought way more than we need."

I am delighted. There are cheese sandwiches, ham sandwiches, chips, breadsticks, chocolate fingers, cupcakes, grapes, apples (one fewer because of the black horse), olives, baby corn, and tomatoes. There's one big bottle of water and three cans of different fizzy drinks.

"How did you fit all this in your backpack?" asks Mom, staring at everything in astonishment.

"With difficulty," he responds, and she laughs. I choke on my baby corn because it's a real laugh, not the fake one. I stare at her in surprise.

"What?" she says.

I eat and eat and there's still food left, and I'm sure Lennon doesn't want to carry too much back so I'm doing him a favor, and Mom eats much more than usual and doesn't mention calories even once.

When we've finished, we all lie back on the blanket and stare at the sky and play the cloud game. "Dragon," says my mom, pointing.

"No way," says Lennon. "That's an elephant dancing."

"No," I argue, "it's a baby in a bath. You can see its head sticking out over the top." I change voices. "Goo goo, 'ook at me. I'm in the bath, oops, I've fallen in, argh argh, noo, I'm drowning . . . !"

It's a *really* lame impression, but Lennon starts laughing, and that makes me laugh, and then Mom giggles, and then Lennon starts coughing, and has to sit up because he can't breathe properly, and then Mom stops giggling because she's really worried about him, but

I keep laughing and laughing because I can't stop and eventually my sides start to ache and *that* seems funny too, and Lennon has stopped coughing and started laughing again because I'm laughing, and I don't know how long it all goes on for but at the end, I feel as though someone has turned me upside down and shaken out all the bad stuff.

I lie on the grass (having laughed myself off the blanket) and stare up at the sky, and my body feels calm and light and warm, and I can almost hear the grass growing and the beetles scuttling and the sun sizzling.

Lennon starts to play his guitar. It's a song I don't know, about questions and answers that are blowing in the wind. It's quite soothing. I close my eyes and lose myself in the song.

And then a second very, very quiet voice joins Lennon's and my eyes jerk open.

My mom is singing.

Chapter 20

"Nearly spring break!" Kayma shouts in the playground as we meet up on Monday. We dance around together, shouting, "Spring break! Spring break! Spring break!"

"You want to come over?" Kayma says, and then adds hopefully, "Or I could come to you."

I pull a face. "I'm going away. Sorry. Vacation-resort thing. It's been booked for ages."

"Oh, noooo," moans Kayma. "That's so unfair. I'm going to be stuck at home all week with Hula. Fliss can't get time off work, and Mom says we can't afford to go anywhere because we have to save all our money for our summer vacation in Corfu. Maybe Sanvi will let me come over."

I try to cheer her up. "What, you don't want to spend time with your adorable baby sister? But she's so cute!" I put on Hula's voice: *"Kayma, what are you doing? Kayma, can I play with you? Kayma, give me all your toys, Mom says you have to!"*

Kayma falls down laughing. "That's exactly what she sounds like!"

Sanvi runs up to us, out of breath. "Oh, I haven't missed the bell. I thought I was late!"

Kayma, still laughing, says, "You have to see this. Jelly, do it again!"

I do my impression of Hula again. Kayma squeals with laughter. Sanvi smiles doubtfully. "That does sound a lot like her. But, I don't know, is it . . . um . . . ?" She shuffles her feet and glances around.

"What?" I ask, in my normal voice. Then I switch back to Hula. *"Oh, come on, tell me! You lot are always leaving me out of things!"*

"I just mean . . . What if she heard you? She'd be really upset."

Panic grips me and I swing around, scanning the

playground quickly. Hula is nowhere to be seen. "She's not here," I say boldly, relieved. If Hula *were* there, I'd feel bad . . . but she isn't. "And anyway, I do impressions of the teachers in front of them all the time."

"Well, actually, you don't," Sanvi points out. "When they come along, you stop and go bright red."

"I do not!" I laugh. "Well, maybe a bit."

"You so do," Kayma agrees. "Like a tomato."

"Or a watermelon," says Sanvi.

"Or a strawberry." Then Kayma remembers what started this conversation. "Sanvi! Can I come over during spring break? Please say I can. I'm going to go *bananas* if I can't get away from Hula." She grips Sanvi's arms so tightly that Sanvi winces.

"Yes, you crazy person! Get off me!"

The bell rings and Kayma repeats "thankyouthank-youthankyou" as we go into school. My tummy feels all knotted up. I do impressions all the time. I'm not being mean, am I? It's only because people are really easy to impersonate. They should find it funny that I've picked up on things they do and say or the way they walk or sniff or rub their nose. A thought occurs to me: Maybe it wouldn't be right to impersonate Hula because she's got a disability? I feel a bit queasy at that. In health class we're told we shouldn't stare at or make fun of people who are different from ourselves. Should I *not* do an impression of Hula simply because she's only got one arm? But she's so *easy* to mimic. . . .

While I'm thinking this, I walk slap bang into Marshall and knock him into the wall by mistake. "Oof!"

"Oh, sorry!" I say.

Marshall swings around, rubbing his shoulder. "Ow, that *really* hurt."

"I said I'm sorry," I say. "I didn't see you."

His lips scrunch up into a scowl. "Can't you look where you're going, Jelly? It's like being hit by a *tank*." Then he turns away and goes into the classroom.

I take several seconds more than I need to hang up my bag because my face is burning with shame. A tank. Because I am bigger and heavier than everyone else. . . .

There's an old saying about sticks and stones. It says they can hurt you but words can't. I don't know who wrote that, but they couldn't be more wrong. Everyone can see the bruises left by sticks and stones. Those bruises fade. The ones left by words are invisible, but they never go away.

I don't feel quite myself for most of the morning. It feels like stuff is churning around inside me. I make a couple of people laugh by doing silly things with pencils, but it's an effort.

And then when I go to the bathroom at break, there's a dark smudge on my underwear.

Chapter 21

I stare at it in panic. Is that . . . ? What *is* that? Am I hurt? Have I cut myself without realizing? It looks like blood, only kind of brown.

Oh.

Oh, no.

No, no, it can't be!

A sudden image of Kayma's room: the *Your Body and Its Changes* book . . . the chapter on . . . *periods*.

Oh, *yuck*. Oh, this is *so* not fair. I glare at my underwear as though it's somehow its fault. This is revolting. I can't believe this is actually a thing that happens to girls. Bleeding, every *month*, out of my . . . YUCKYUCKYUCK, I can't even *think* it! I'm only *eleven*!

Angrily, I thump my fist against the cubicle wall. "Hey!" comes a voice from the next cubicle. "What's that for?"

"Sorry!" I blurt out. "Slipped!"

Panic sweeps over me like a cold shower. What am I meant to do? I haven't got any . . . *things*. Any plastic-wrapped squares or tubes like my mom has. I don't think I'd even know what to do with one. Some public toilets have machines where you can buy them—but there's nothing like that here at school. And I haven't got any money anyway.

How much . . . blood . . . will there be? If I just wait and don't do anything, will it go right through my skirt? Will I end up sitting in a brown-red puddle? I'm paralyzed by fright, imagining everyone pointing and laughing at me. I'd never live it down.

I feel a bit dizzy. The book said it was a big moment, the first time. It shows a girl has become a woman. Am I suddenly a *woman*? Is that why I feel like I'm going to throw up?

A loud banging on the toilet door makes me jump in fright. "Are you all right in there?"

I can't speak. There are murmurings outside the door. "Who's in there?"

"I dunno, but she's been ages."

"Maybe she's doing a poo." Much giggling.

"Maybe she's fainted. My sister said once there was a girl who fainted in the toilets at her school and the teacher had to break open the door and put her in the recovery position."

"There was that bang a few minutes ago. I was right next to her, nearly made me pee my pants."

More giggling.

"No, but maybe she hit her head?"

"She said she slipped. Maybe she passed out after that. Can you get delayed unconscious?"

"Should we get someone?"

"Look under the door. See if she's lying on the floor."

Hastily I grab a wad of toilet paper and stuff it into my underwear.

"I can hear the toilet roll going," someone outside says. "She's not unconscious."

"Maybe she's crying. Hello, are you all right in there?"

"I already asked that, but she didn't answer."

"I'm a Bullying Ambassador. Maybe I should try to talk to her. Er . . . hello in there. Is there anything the matter?"

"How is that any different from what *I* said?"

"If you ask someone if they're all right, all they can say is yes or no."

"You can say that to 'is anything the matter?' too."

I flush the toilet and unlock the door. Three girls fall into the cubicle.

"Oh," says one of them, "it's you! Are you OK?"

"I'm fine!" I say, as though surprised to be asked. "Why wouldn't I be?"

The girls exchange glances. "You were in there for ages."

"Oh," I say, brain racing, "I was, like, writing a comedy sketch in my head."

"What?"

"Yeah . . ." I warm to my lie. "I was just thinking about Mrs. Belize and Ms. Jones meeting at the dentist, and Mrs. Belize has just had a filling and her face is all numb, and she can't speak properly, so she's like, 'Hewwo, Mtth Joneth, what a thurprithe,' and Ms. Jones is leaning back because Mrs. Belize is dribbling everywhere."

The girls are laughing now.

"I was in *there* so long," I say, waving at the toilet, "because I was so busy thinking up stuff I forgot to get off."

"My brother takes his phone to the bathroom," one of the girls says. "He can be in there for *hours*."

This sparks an enthusiastic conversation between the girls about what people take with them to the bathroom and the longest one of them has ever had to wait, and the time Hetty Callaghan peed all over the floor because the toilets were all occupied. I push past them to wash my hands and leave them to it.

You know how sometimes time speeds up? This is not one of those times. Every single minute that goes by feels like an hour. At lunchtime I rush back to the toilet to change the wad of toilet roll. There isn't as much . . . stuff . . . as I'd expected. Which is a relief but doesn't make me any less paranoid for the rest of the day. And the tissue in my pants makes me wriggle uncomfortably.

Do you ever get this weird desire to shout out something completely inappropriate? Like when you all have to be dead quiet in assembly, and you just want to shout

"BIG HAIRY BUTTS" or something, and you have to swallow it down because although it would be hilarious for about half a second, you know you'd go bright red afterward and be seriously told off?

Well, that. I spend the whole afternoon biting back "I AM BLEEDING DOWN THERE," but because I'm not very good at being quiet, I make up for it by being super-silly and annoying. I know I'm doing it, but I can't stop because I'm worried that if I try to sit quietly, the embarrassing words will burst out of me like a fountain and then everyone will stare at me and screw up their noses in disgust and I'll end up crying on the floor and *never be able to go back to school again.*

"Angelica," Mr. Lenck says, more than once, "be quiet, please."

But I can't. He frowns and starts to make a mark on the board next to my name every time he has to speak to me. "Get to five, and you'll lose break time," he warns me.

I scrape to the end of the day on four warnings and when the bell rings, I start to laugh hysterically. No one knew! No one guessed! I go out into the hall and do an extra-funny version of Mrs. Belize at the dentist for Kayma and Sanvi. They fall about laughing. "That's brilliant," Kayma says, wiping her eyes. "You have to put that in your K Factor act."

"Do you think?" I ask.

"Well . . ." says Sanvi, cautious as ever, "Mrs. Belize will be watching, so maybe it's not such a good idea to make fun of her. . . ."

"I could change it," I say, "so that it's more about the dentist. Oh, I know! How about I make it that Mr. Lenck is the dentist! And Mrs. Belize is totally shocked to see him and he says this is my second job because everyone knows teaching doesn't pay well enough, so I'm being a dentist part-time—and she says, 'Are you qualified?' And he says, 'I've done a four-day course and I'm really good with a drill.' And Mrs. Belize faints on the floor!"

Sanvi is nodding along, her eyes shining. "That sounds *very* funny," she says. "Much better!"

"Cool!" I turn to grab my bag.

"Oh, hang on a minute," Sanvi says, bending down. "You've got something stuck to the back of your skirt . . . oh! What's *that*?"

I feel like someone's tipped a bucket of iced water over

me. I twist out of her grasp, pulling at my skirt with my hand. "Oh, nothing. I sat in some chocolate earlier," I lie. "Mom's going to kill me."

"Oh, dear." Sanvi loses interest. "See you in the morning, yeah?"

"Yep." I wave them off, then carefully tie my cardigan around my waist so that no one can see the back of my skirt. Then, trembling, I set off for home. Mom will help. I can talk to her.

But when I open the door to my apartment and go into the living room to dump my bags, the only person there, sitting in the armchair and strumming his guitar, is Lennon.

Chapter 22

"Hey, Jelly," Lennon says, smiling at me. "What's new with you today?"

"What do you mean?" I say sharply. "Nothing's new."

He looks surprised. "Oh, sorry, I didn't mean it to sound weird. Don't you hate it when people say, 'How was school?' I was just trying to ask something different."

"Where's Mom?" I ask abruptly.

He nods toward the hallway. "In her room, on the phone, with the door shut. Something's happened at HQ. I'm not sure if it's good or bad, but it's all very intense and she's been in there fifteen minutes already."

He frowns slightly. "Are you all right? You look stressed. Has something happened?"

I don't know what to do. Something weird is definitely happening to me right now. I stare at him, and I feel hot and cold and fuzzy, and a bit sick. The edges of my vision start to darken.

Lennon jumps up. "Jelly, sit down. You need to—" But I don't hear what he says next.

When I open my eyes I'm on the floor. It's very peculiar. Why am I on the floor?

Lennon is sitting cross-legged next to me. He says, "Hello! You fainted."

"What?" I still feel fuzzy, and my body is heavy and tired. I don't feel any desire to move.

"You fainted. My last girlfriend used to do it quite a lot, so I could tell you were about to. Don't worry, I think you're all right. You didn't hit your head or anything. It was quite a graceful faint. Did you eat lunch today? My girlfriend used to faint when she hadn't eaten enough."

"Er . . ." I try to think. "I ate lunch." I don't remember what it was, but I'm sure I ate lunch. I always eat lunch.

"That's good," he says. "It might take you a few minutes to feel better. It's OK—you can stay on the floor."

Suddenly I feel very silly. I sit up.

"Don't try anything too quickly," Lennon warns me. "You might faint again."

"I'm not going to faint again. I've never fainted before." It wasn't at all how I thought fainting would feel.

"I'll go and get your mom," Lennon says, unfolding his long legs. "I didn't want to leave the room while you were unconscious."

"No—no, don't bother her." Mom isn't good with illnesses. She always gets really worried and starts fussing. I don't want fussing right now. "Don't interrupt her. I'm fine. I'll talk to her in a bit."

Lennon tilts his head to one side. "You sure? You still look quite pale."

"I'll just sit here for a bit." I wriggle my legs around to be more comfortable.

"You've got something on your skirt," Lennon comments.

I freeze.

This may be the single most embarrassing thing that has ever happened to me. I don't know what to do. "It's chocolate," I blurt out.

Lennon's eyebrows *boing* upward at my sharp and

instant response. "Oh," he says. And then there's a pause, and my gaze drops to the carpet and my face burns red. After a long, long moment, Lennon says nicely, "Jelly, do you want to go to the bathroom?"

"Yes," I gulp out, and I get up and stagger out of the room.

I dump my skirt and underwear in the bath. Mom will know what to do with them. Then I rummage through the bathroom cabinet and take out one of the plastic-wrapped squares from Mom's stash. I tie a towel around my waist and scuttle to my room, where I attempt to stick the pad to a clean pair of underwear. It's way harder than I thought. I have to keep un-peeling it and resticking it, and then I accidentally stick it to my . . . er . . . *you know*, and yelp with pain. Why didn't we have a lesson on *these* at school? This is going to take a lot of practice.

By the time I'm dressed and sorted, I'm feeling frustrated and wobbly. Is this what made me faint? Is this why my tummy felt weird all morning?

I hesitate outside Mom's bedroom. She's *still* on the phone. Fragments of the conversation float through the door. ". . . get what you're saying, but it's not exactly fair of them, is it? I mean . . . last one in, first one out.

How long before the rest of us are at risk? I don't know, Cass, maybe it's time to . . . yeah, me too. Not that easy though, is it, finding something that fits around the kids?"

My hand, which was on the doorknob, drops away. This isn't a conversation I can interrupt. Mom sounds stressed.

"Jelly?" Lennon appears at the end of the hallway, waving an empty mug. "Hot chocolate?"

I smile. "It's, like, seventy degrees outside."

"So? Hot chocolate is what you give girls at that time of the month. Preferably with a side helping of *actual* chocolate. Or ice cream, if push comes to shove. That's what I've always been told. Which of the three do you want? I guess it's more ice-cream weather."

I'm not a big one for ice cream normally, but today it sounds like a really good idea. Together we rummage through the freezer and unearth a tub of salted caramel. Lennon hands me the whole thing, with a spoon. "I believe the thing to do is to eat it straight from the tub," he says, "while complaining about the unfairness of being female. Do you want a hot water bottle?"

I can't help but laugh. "It's *boiling* outside."

He shakes his head. "Hey, I never said it made sense."

Then he smiles and sits down next to me at the table. "What do you usually do for it?"

I dig into the solid ice cream. "It's my first time."

"No way! You poor thing. No wonder you look like you've seen a ghost. Bit of a shock?"

I nod, not looking at him.

"Happened at school, did it?"

"This morning. I didn't tell anyone."

"You should probably eat the whole tub," he says kindly, which makes me laugh again. "Hey, listen, I keep meaning to ask for my harmonica back. I've got a gig coming up next week and I need it for a couple of the songs. Is that OK?"

"Oh. Yeah, of course."

"You can borrow it back again afterward," he says. "If you want."

"OK."

He looks at me curiously. "Jelly," he says, "don't take this the wrong way, but . . . is there something the matter? I mean, apart from what's happened today? Are you worried about something?"

I lick ice cream off the spoon, cleaning every last bit. "Um . . . no . . ." I say.

"It's just that . . ." He pauses. "You said once you write

poems. I wondered—it reminded me of what I said about writing music to express things I couldn't say to people. Does it . . . do you . . . are there things you can't say to people that you want to? Are you maybe pretending to be something you're not, to fit in with other people?"

I stare at the tub of ice cream. I want to laugh it off, tell him I'm fine, crack a joke—maybe even do an impression of him looking all serious.

I don't do any of those things. Instead I get up, go to my bedroom, pull out the pink book from under my pillow, come back, and put the book on the table.

"Phew," he says. "I thought I'd offended you there. Wow. Is this your poetry?"

I nod.

"Are you sure it's OK for me to look at? You don't have to share it, you know."

I shrug and sit down. Somehow I've lost the ability to speak.

He picks up the book and starts to flip through it. I see his gaze travel from side to side as he reads the lines. A range of expressions flickers across his face. I watch him as he reads my inner thoughts.

"Wow," he says after a few pages. "These are really, really good, Jelly."

I don't know what I was expecting him to say, but it wasn't that.

"They really are. You have a gift with words. This one here, about hiding behind lies—'Is this me? Is this you?'—it's got a real rhythm to it, a musicality. In fact . . ." He pauses for a moment, and then takes another breath. "In fact, would you mind . . . could I borrow this poem? I just . . . it sings to me. I want to set it to music."

My jaw drops. "Really?"

"It's stunning, you know. Lyrics are so hard to write. They're the thing that takes me longest, and you—you just breathe them, it seems. They pour out of you. How long have you been writing these?"

"Er . . . well, I got that book last Christmas."

"So these are all from the last six months?" He shakes his head, incredulous, and flips the pages of my book. "That's amazing. There are so many poems in here. You must write every day!"

"Not quite every day," I say.

He opens the book to his favorite poem again. "What do you think?"

"You want to borrow the book?" I say, unsure. I need that book.

"Oh, no," he says hastily. "I can take a photo of this

one. But only if it's all right with you."

I'm such a mix of feelings I don't know what to do, except shrug and say, "I guess—yeah, go ahead." He pulls out his phone and snaps a photo of the pages. Then he closes my book and slides it across the table toward me. "Thank you for sharing it with me," he says. "I'm really honored, honest."

I hear the sound of Mom's bedroom door opening suddenly, and I snatch the book off the table and sit on it quickly.

". . . oughtn't to be allowed to get away with it," she's saying angrily, and then sees me. "Hello, love. I'm so sorry. I was caught up in something." She gives me a hug and I can smell a new perfume, something floral with a sharp citrus tang. "The company is reducing its number of agents so that we get to cover a wider area. Which is good news for me because I pick up more clients, but poor Maisie only signed up a month ago and they've revoked her license and she's in tears, and I feel terrible about it." She stops to draw a breath and adds, "I need a green tea."

Lennon gets up. "I'll make it," he says. "Jelly has something to tell you."

My eyes widen in alarm. He's not talking about the

poetry, surely? I thought he knew it was private!

"About what happened to her today at school," he continues, giving me a reassuring wink.

I breathe out again in relief.

Mom sits down. "Something happened to you? Are you all right?" She looks down at the tub as though noticing it for the first time. "Have you been eating ice cream?"

"I started my period today," I say, and the words seem to fall from my lips quite easily, as though it's a perfectly normal thing to say, to anyone, at any time.

Mom gasps. "Oh, my goodness! Are you sure? That's—oh, my little Jelly!" She leaps up and comes round to throw her arms around me.

My little Jelly makes me simultaneously want to laugh and do a fake puke. But I like the hug and I hug her back. The new perfume slides up my nose and makes me want to sneeze.

"I can't believe it!" Mom says, stroking my hair and cupping my face so she can look at me. "My little girl is growing up!" Her eyes fill with tears. "Are you OK? Did they sort you out with something at school?"

"Er . . ." I say. "Not exactly. I . . . um . . . I used toilet paper."

Mom laughs tearfully. "I did exactly the same thing!" She blushes suddenly as she sees Lennon standing in the doorway. "Oh, goodness—you don't want to be hearing all this girl stuff."

He says, "It's fine."

"He got the ice cream out for me," I point out.

"You did?" Mom stares at him. "Well, that's . . . wow. That's nice of you."

"I offered hot chocolate and a hot water bottle too," he says, "but they were rejected."

Mom laughs in a kind of astonished way. "It seems I've finally met a man who isn't weirded out by this stuff."

"She fainted too," he comments. "When she first got home."

"*What*?" Mom turns to me and immediately starts looking in my eyes and feeling my forehead and all the things people do when you're ill. "You fainted? Lennon, why didn't you come and get me?"

"I didn't want to leave her unsupervised," he says.

"Oh. Oh—well, all right, I can see why. . . ." She frowns at me. "How are you feeling now?"

"Fine," I say. "I left my things in the bath," I add in a lowered voice. "I didn't know what to do with them."

"I'll put them in to soak," she says, with a smile.

"Don't worry, I'll sort it out. Did you find what you needed?"

"Yes, I took one of yours."

She gives me a very tight squeeze, so tight that it almost hurts, and kisses me on the top of my head. "I've got a grown-up daughter!" she says. "I feel so *old*!" Then she goes off to the bathroom.

Changes

Life is a straight line
divided into dashes
chopped by events
an existence neatly sliced.

That was yesterday
Things are different now
you can't go back
From today you start
a new line
until this one is also

snipped

and there will be another
                    tomorrow
and a sealed-off
                    yesterday

Chapter 23

I love our time at the resort over spring break. There are activities laid out, from surfing to glass painting to archery, and best of all there's an all-you-can-eat buffet every evening with a massive range of options. They do pizza, curry, casserole, roast, chicken nuggets, pasta. . . . Every day I go swimming and running and dancing, and every evening I take a plate and load it up with all my favorite things. Mom has smoked mackerel and quinoa and arugula and a glass of wine, and we are happy as anything. We both miss Lennon quite a lot, but we FaceTime him a couple of times, and he sends Mom a new song he's been working on.

I wonder if he's started work on the song from my poem, but I can't say anything to Mom about it because then she'd ask about my poetry and I still don't want her to know. Somehow showing the book to Lennon is different from showing it to Mom. It feels less scary.

I like the resort for another reason: The people there are all sizes, and lots of them are kind of big. I'm not the fattest kid in the place by a *long* way; in fact, I feel almost thin. There are whole families of really fat people. And they're all having a great time, so nobody cares what size anyone is.

I make friends with a girl named Keris. She's got curly hair and a round smiley face and is exactly the same size as me—I know this because one day we decide to swap clothes for the evening disco, and her dress fits me perfectly. We dance for a whole hour without stopping, and we persuade our moms to buy us lemonade and a bag of popcorn and Chex Mix, and it's the happiest I've felt for ages.

We're away for five whole days, and in all that time, I don't write in my poetry book once.

On the last Saturday of spring break, Lennon comes for the afternoon to take Mom out to dinner. He's brought his guitar, and he winks at me when he sees me. I am filled with excitement but also panic. How can I get Mom out of the way so he can play the song?

Lennon takes the decision out of my hands. "Got another new song to play you both," he says, unzipping the guitar case.

"Another one?" asks Mom. "You *have* been busy!"

"This one's different," he tells her. "You have a listen and see what you think."

My hands prickle with sweat as he tunes up and pauses, placing his fingers on the frets. Then he begins, a picked little melody to start with . . .

Is this me? Is this you?
Is this the best that we can do?
Hiding behind a web of lies
Hoping you can't see in my eyes
Tell a joke, be a clown
Don't let you see when I am down
Keep all my worries deep inside
Don't let you know I cried

Cos I'm a happy face
Hiding an empty space

Yes I'm a happy face
But if you could see beyond the smile
Would you still be there?
Would you want to be my friend,
Would you even care?
Cos I'm a happy face
Hiding an empty space

Life is cool, life is fun
That's what I tell everyone
Nothing you say can hurt me, see?

That's my identity
Cos I'm a happy face
Hiding an empty space
Yes, I'm a happy face

But if you could see beyond the smile
Would you still be there?
Would you want to be my friend,
Would you even care?
Cos I'm a happy face
Hiding an empty space

And if you could see beyond the smile
Would you still be there?

Would you want to be my friend,
Would you even care?
Cos I'm a happy face
Hiding an empty space
Yes I'm a happy face
Hiding an empty space
Being a big disgrace
To the whole human race
Keeping my smile in place
Remember my happy face

I listen, spellbound. He's changed some of my words around and added more to make it longer and fit the structure of the song. In the middle there's a little bit where he hums a melody before singing the chorus again. And the melody seems to just fit the meaning behind the words. Melancholy and sad but sounding kind of bright and cheerful every now and then, as though it's fooling itself.

The last notes die away, and I can't quite speak. Lennon looks up to meet my gaze and tips his head on one side, as though asking me if I approve. I try to smile, but have to settle for nodding hard.

Mom sniffs, and I realize there are tears on her face. "Oh, goodness," she says, trying to dab them away without ruining her mascara. "That's so sad. You do write such beautiful lyrics."

"Actually these lyrics aren't mine," Lennon says. "They're by . . . um . . . a friend."

"Then I just want to give your friend a big hug," says Mom, doing one of those emotional laughs that aren't quite amusement or misery. "He sounds like he needs it."

I press my lips together very hard. *It's me*, I want to say. *I wrote it.* I'm the one who's pretending everything's fine when, underneath, it's not. I hate how people judge me for the way I look. I hate how I can't tell anyone it bothers me. Most of all, I hate that I've created a version of myself that I can't step away from, because it's too scary to let people see how I really feel.

But I can't say it, even to Mom.

I know Lennon knows, and I'm glad I trusted him. I know he'll keep my secret.

"It's a beautiful song," I say in the end, when I've gotten control over my voice.

"You know that bit in the middle," he says, "where I was humming? I was thinking it would work really well on harmonica. Do you think you'd like to learn it?"

I could play on my own song? That's . . . awesome. "Yeah," I say, beaming at him.

"Good," he says, "because I brought you something." From his bag, he pulls out a small box. And I know just what's in there. "I asked your mom," he says, passing it to me, "if it was OK to give you a present. It's not a fantastic-quality one. But it should do the job."

I've had lots of presents over the years. Mom usually buys me makeup or clothes or handbags or shoes. Cute T-shirts, pretty skirts, glittered sneakers, that kind of thing. Nan and Grandpa have always given me books, though they're stuck in the past, so none of the books are ever the ones I would choose to read for myself. Auntie Maggi tends to send me parcels of whatever she's been given for free.

But this is a musical instrument. No one's ever given me one of these before.

I open the box and stare at the shiny silver object. It's much shinier than the one Lennon lent me. I guess his must be quite old now.

"I thought it was better to have one for yourself," Lennon says. "Rather than having to borrow mine all the time."

"Say thank you," Mom nudges me.

"Thank you," I say, stroking the harmonica like it's a small pet. "Thank you very much."

He smiles. "No problem. Shall I teach you the tune for the middle bit of the song?"

I don't mind that Mom and Lennon go out for dinner without me. I don't mind Rosie coming and slumping on the sofa, her thumbs flying over the surface of her phone screen as usual. To be honest, I'm quite glad for the space to be on my own, in my room, just . . . breathing in everything. My words have become a *song*. That's . . . that's amazing. I open my poetry book, but for once I don't know how to start.

Instead I pick up the harmonica. It feels different against my mouth from the other one. It has a different tone too. This one sounds . . . sweeter, maybe.

I practice the melody from the middle of my song. *My song*. No one's ever written me a song before. I want to hear it again, but we didn't record it. I'm upset about that. I should have asked Lennon. Maybe I could ask him to record it when he and Mom get back. . . . No, it'll be late. That would be ridiculous.

I go to the living room to tell Rosie I'm going to bed, but I see the back of her head over the top of the sofa and I know she's got her earphones in and is messaging or beautifying selfies or whatever and I don't want to interrupt her, so I just go back to my room.

I open my book to the page with the original version of my poem, and I realize I don't know if Lennon gave my song a title. I hum it in my head, trying to remember the extra lyrics he wrote. I should have asked him to write them down for me. I'll get Mom to ask him when I see her in the morning.

I lie in bed and stare at the ceiling. Usually I don't feel all that great when I'm going to sleep. Things I've said during the day, a sideways comment from someone at school, that extra Twix I took from the cupboard that I shouldn't have had . . . everything congeals into a soup of negative feelings and eventually I fall asleep exhausted from the stuff I can't talk to anyone about.

Tonight I fall asleep with a song in my head and my heart.

Chapter 24

I am *on fire* at The K Factor auditions! The first round is held in our classrooms, so I only have to perform for my friends, but I have to impress everyone enough to make them vote for me. Only the two acts with the most votes from each class will go through to the final, and the adrenaline whizzes through my body, making me sharper and funnier than ever.

I've worked hard on the new material about Mrs. Belize going to the dentist, and it goes down like *wildfire*! Everyone is laughing. Will Matsunaga laughs so hard he falls off his chair. Even Mr. Lenck can't stop laughing as I do an impression of him holding a drill, saying, "I couldn't take the stress anymore! Now I never have to deal with the superintendent again! Don't worry—I've watched lots of instructional videos on YouTube. I know *exactly* what I'm doing. Hold still—it's your own time you're wasting!"

Cheering breaks out at the end of my performance. People slap me on the back as I make my way to my seat. Kayma, still giggling, says, "You've got this in the *bag*, Jelly!"

Not everyone in our class auditions. Some people don't like performing, others just haven't got their act together in time. Marshall does a magic trick that would have worked if he'd hidden the colored scarves up his sleeve a bit better. Avalon plays the violin and I try not to flinch. Two of the girls do an awkward gymnastics routine, which isn't easy in the classroom, and Will does a beatbox thing, which is surprisingly good. Kayma and Sanvi sing their song, and poor Sanvi forgets half the words to the second verse, so I clap extra-enthusiastically at the end to show it didn't matter (it did, of course). "I can't believe I messed it up!" she says miserably as she sits back down. "I *know* the words! I got too nervous. I'm so sorry, Kayma."

"It's not your fault," Kayma tells her, but I can see she's disappointed.

"It wasn't that bad," I reassure her. "I bet most people didn't even notice."

We vote at the end, writing down the names of the two acts we liked best. The vote is anonymous, so Mr. Lenck says we can vote for ourselves, since he won't be able to check. So of course I vote for myself, and for Kayma and Sanvi, out of loyalty.

"Thank you," says Mr. Lenck, collecting all the slips of paper. "I'll announce the top two winners tomorrow morning." Loud groans break out at this. "Those are the rules!" he exclaims. "All the classes will announce at the same time."

"Whaaaaaat??" Marshall falls to the floor dramatically. "I'll die from anticipation!"

"Marshall, I don't know *what* you think you're doing," says Mr. Lenck drily. "Get up. I'm about to give out a math sheet."

"Then I may as well be dead!" cries Marshall.

"Me too!" I cry, and slump forward across my table, making a groaning sound. A ripple effect sets off everyone in the classroom doing fake deaths, and it takes Mr. Lenck several minutes to get control again. Marshall high-fives me as he's sent back to his chair.

As we collect our bags at the end of the day, Kayma says to me confidentially, "You're *in*, Jelly. A hundred and ten percent."

"What?" I say, glancing around. "How do you know?"

"Cos I've been asking everyone who they voted for," she says with a grin. "You're in the lead by *miles*."

Of course, it's not actually confirmed until tomorrow, but I walk home feeling really good about myself. I even shout out a hello to the man with the harmonica who's in the park again, playing another sad tune. "Play something happy!" I call. He looks surprised, and then breaks into something by Beyoncé, which sounds *really* odd on harmonica, I can tell you.

"Hello, gorgeous!" says Mom as soon as I come in the door. She's wearing a thin, floaty summer dress with poppies on it and she has a huge smile on her face. She looks amazing.

"Hi!" I say, smiling back.

She gets up from the dining table with something in her hand. "Fancy going shopping?" she asks, showing me a fistful of dollars.

I beam. "Now? Yes!"

I quickly get changed, and we start walking into

town. "A big order came in," she explains. I look into Coffeetastic as we pass in case I need to wave at Fliss, but I can't see her. "This woman is having a bachelorette party, and she wants to give all the girls coming a beauty box. She's absolutely *loaded*, this woman. I mean, she's ordered, like, twelve of everything: foundations, eye shadow palettes, lipsticks, serums, all sorts. It's bonkers what people will spend on their weddings." She sounds a bit wistful.

I glance at her. "Do you want to get married, Mom?"

She gives a sort of half laugh. "Oh, well, I don't know. You know, there's something nice about the . . . the whole idea, isn't there? I wouldn't mind getting to wear the white dress and all that. The fairy tale." The smile slides off her lips and she shrugs. "Fairy tales aren't real life though."

I wait for a moment and then I say, "Would you marry Lennon if he asked you?"

Her eyes flick straight to me, as though I've said something really shocking. "*Lennon*? What makes you say that?" Her voice trembles a bit.

"I just wondered. He's really nice, Mom."

"Yes, he is, but . . . marriage is a big thing, Jelly."

"I know that. I was just wondering."

"Well, don't," she says almost sharply. "There's no use in wondering. Things are either meant to be, or they're not. Wondering doesn't change anything."

I don't say anything else until we reach the shops. "I think it's time for some new outfits," says Mom, and we head straight into H&M. I love new clothes. There's something about so many colors and fabrics all in one place that makes me a bit loopy. I grab things off racks that I know won't really suit me, but they look so pretty hanging there that I have to try them!

"Six items maximum," says the lady at the changing-room doors. She smiles at me. "I think you might have more like fifteen there."

"Sorry." I count out six and hand over the others for her to keep aside for me. "I love this shop."

"Well, that's nice to know," she says cheerfully before separating out six items from Mom's arms too.

In the cubicle, I pull on a nice pair of black pants and then frown. They won't go up around my waist. Sighing, I start to push them down again, when the curtain twitches aside and Mom comes in. "Look at this!" she says excitedly. She's wearing a lovely white tunic top with little holes in it, like you'd make from a hole punch.

It looks great on her. "Oh, those pants look nice—pull them up so I can see."

"No," I say, struggling to get them past my knees. "They're the wrong size."

"Wrong size?" She frowns. "Turn around."

Before I can stop her, she's twisted me around so she can reach the label at the back. "But this is your usual size," she says. "What's wrong with them?"

"They don't suit me," I say, feeling a rising panic. "I just don't like them."

"Show me."

There's no choice. Heat burning in my face, I slide the pants back up. Even if I suck in really far, I can't do up the button.

"Oh," she says quietly. "Oh, that's . . . Oh, Jelly." She is staring at my tummy, and I can't bear it.

I push down the pants so hard the plastic tag scratches my thigh, but I don't care. Tears sting my eyes. "I *told* you they didn't suit me."

She reaches out to hug me, but I pull back, losing my balance and stumbling against the wall. "You *know* I hate shopping!" I say fiercely, which is a total lie, but the angry dark cloud in my stomach is twisting my words.

"Why did you even bring me here?"

Mom takes a breath as though she's about to speak, but then she turns and goes back out, pulling the curtain closed behind her. I stare with blurred vision at the brown-and-cream stripes and my knees feel weak, and I reach out to the side of the cubicle to steady myself, because I think I might fall down otherwise.

Then I see myself in the full-length mirror. Why do they make changing-room lights so harsh? I stare bitterly at my hips, my stomach, my thighs, all round and squidgy. I turn sideways and study the tops of my arms. Even the top I'm trying on is pulled tight across my chest. The clothes are the right size and shape for someone my age. But I am not the right size or shape for the clothes.

I have always been the wrong shape, ever since I was little. In baby photos, you can see I'm just a pudge. My bare baby feet are almost square blocks. When babies start to walk, they're supposed to stretch out, become leaner. I didn't. "Such a good eater," everyone cooed over me. I remember people saying it to me. I even remember Nan and Grandpa saying it. Before Grandpa started to point out that I was "chubby" and "too fond of my food."

It's so unfair. Verity Hughes eats *loads*, and yet she stays as thin as a stick figure. It's not as though I'm unfit either. I can run, I'm good at soccer, I'm in Level Four swimming. So why is everything too tight? Why do I have to look for clothes that are for older girls just so I can get into them? Why doesn't elastic stretch farther?

And more than anything, I think, as I stare at myself and the tears stream down my face, more than anything, I wish I didn't have to be the funny one. Making everyone laugh so that they don't notice how fat I am. Fat. Fat. Fat. If they're laughing *with* me, they can't be laughing *at* me, right? And I couldn't bear it if they laughed at me. Or, worse, found me disgusting. I know that's what they really think. And that's why I am the funny one.

If I'm not funny, no one will like me.

Chapter 25

"I waved at you," Kayma says the next morning in the playground. "Outside H&M yesterday afternoon, but you didn't see me. Did you get anything?"

Images flash through my mind: the black pants that wouldn't go up, my shame, running out of the shop (leaving all the other items on the hook untried), the changing-room woman openmouthed, Mom racing after me and trying to talk to me. For once I couldn't laugh it off. For once I couldn't use Option Two. It was terrifying. I felt raw and naked and exposed. Mom didn't know what to do because I wouldn't talk to her, and when I got home I shut myself in my room and cried soundlessly for half an hour. When I finally came out, she made me a cup of tea and gave me a Mars bar to cheer me up.

That was yesterday. Today I am Jelly again, the one everyone knows.

Only half a second passes before I reply to Kayma. "Nah, couldn't find anything I liked. Sorry I didn't see you. I was probably thinking about this new idea for a sketch, where Ms. Jones is trying to teach the Queen how to Hula-Hoop, and the corgis keep getting under her feet."

Sanvi giggles. "That sounds brilliant."

"Does it have to be the Queen?" asks Kayma. "Everyone does the Queen. Maybe . . . er . . . maybe a pop star? Can you do Lady Gaga?"

"I don't know," I reply. "Does she have dogs though? Because it's not funny without the dogs."

We're still discussing this while we head into the classroom, but as soon as Mr. Lenck comes in everyone quiets down immediately because we know he's going to announce the two winners. Mr. Lenck makes us wait *ages* while he takes attendance, and I start to fidget. He glares at me. "I don't know what you think you're doing, Angelica Waters, but I'd like it if you kindly stopped doing it."

"I've got ants in my pants," I say, making everyone laugh. "Aren't you going to tell us who won?"

"If you insist on asking, I'll make you wait until after lunch," Mr. Lenck says acerbically.

Instantly people start hissing at me, "Shut up, Jelly!"

I fall silent, gazing at Mr. Lenck with intense anticipation.

"Right," he says, folding up the attendance sheet. "Now, The K Factor. It was close, you know. Very close."

My heart thuds and I gulp. Have I just missed out? Maybe the gymnastics girls were more popular than I realized?

"We do have two winners," Mr. Lenck continues, "and I have them right here." He holds up a piece of paper. I can't stop wriggling.

"The first person going through to the final," Mr. Lenck says, "is . . . Will Matsunaga, for his beatboxing act."

I clap and cheer along with the rest of the class. Will looks embarrassed and proud all at the same time.

"And the second person going through . . ." Mr. Lenck

pauses, with a slight smirk, "though I hope she won't take it as a signal that she can shout out in class even more . . ."

Yesssss! It's me! I don't even hear him say my name because inside I'm already doing a jig. The class is cheering and I can't stop grinning, and for the whole of the rest of the day people come up to me and slap me on the back and say, "Good old Jelly! I voted for you!"

Good old Jelly. Yessss. Indeedy.

I'm still beaming when I get home, and to my great delight Lennon is on the sofa with Mom. They spring apart when I come in, but I hardly notice, because I'm already shouting, "Guess what, guess what! Guess who got to the final of The K Factor?" Then I dump my bags and do some twerking. "Oh yeah, oh yeah, oh yeah . . ."

Mom leaps up. "That's amazing! I'm so proud of you!"

Lennon comes and gives me a hug too. "Well done. They liked your impressions then?"

"They *loved* them," I say. "Will Matsunaga laughed so hard he fell off his chair!"

Lennon beams at me. "Clever you." He suddenly breaks into a song I don't know: "*Make 'em laaaaff, make 'em laaaaff . . .*" He does jazz hands and everything, and even though I don't know the song and neither does Mom, we both join in with "*laaaaaff*" and do jazz hands and impressions of tap dancing, and for a moment it is . . .

. . . like a family.

And the moment I think that, my stomach drops with nerves. Because I've never had this before. Family has always been just me and Mom, and we didn't need anyone else, or at least I never really thought we did, but now. . . .

You can cut a pizza
into six pieces
or eight
or ten
(if it's big enough)
but it's still
the same amount of pizza

I thought my heart
was like a pizza
It had slices for my friends
and a big slice for my mom
a slice for Aunt Maggi
and one for Nan
(though none for Grandad)

I thought it was already
divided up
but somehow
Lennon is in there now too
and the funny thing is
the other slices haven't got
any smaller

So that means
that my heart

must have

got bigger

"Jelly." Lennon knocks at my door. "I'm heading off in a minute, but can I talk to you?"

For one weird whirlwind of a wish, I wonder if he's about to ask me if he can marry my mom.

I pause, the poetry book half shoved under my pillow. "Um . . . yeah."

He comes in, closing the door behind him. This is definitely weird. He glances around and then folds his legs under him to sit on the floor. "I wanted to say I think it's really amazing about you getting through to the final of this talent-show thing."

"Thanks."

"Do people . . . ?"

He stops, and it's like he's trying to work out what to say next. "Does anyone . . . ? Can you change your act, once you're through to the final?"

I stare at him. "What do you mean?" Inside, my tummy aches a little that this isn't about marrying my mom.

"Well," he says slowly, "I was just thinking, the talent show would be a fantastic opportunity for you to perform one of your poems. Or maybe . . . do your song."

My eyes widen. "*What*?"

He rushes on, because he knows I'm about to object,

very loudly and firmly. "Listen, just hear me out. I know you hide a lot of yourself away, under this jolly outside. I get it: I totally see why you need to do that. It's like a survival mechanism. But . . . thing is, it's not who you really are, the girl who cracks jokes all the time. You're *way* more than that, Jelly. You're smart and clever and you *feel* things, and you have a real talent for writing, such a way with words. You're so expressive, and nobody sees it. I don't think you know quite how unusual you are, to be able to write poetry like you do. To be so self-aware at your age, to be able to see behind faces and pretenses and look at life and the world in that way . . . it's extraordinary, you know? You're pretty unique. And I think . . . maybe the world should see it. You. The other Jelly."

I find my voice at last. "I can't."

"I know how it feels," Lennon says. "Sometimes I write a song and, when I sing it, it feels like I'm exposing everything inside me. It's inviting people in to see what I'm really like, bad thoughts and stupid mistakes and all. And, even more frightening, people can see what I hope for and long for." He falls silent for a moment, and then says, "Anyway, this isn't about me. If you did do your song in the talent show, I'd come along and play guitar for you. And sing with you, if it would make you feel better. And think: Everyone could hear you playing the harmonica too! You've got so good at it, and I bet you haven't shared it, have you?"

I shake my head. I can't speak.

"Will you think about it at least?" Lennon asks. "When is the final anyway?"

"Next week," I say, in a voice that sounds faint and faraway. "Friday evening."

He nods. There is silence again. After a few moments he gets to his feet and says, "You don't have to, of course. You can go on and do your impressions, and it sounds like you might even win, you're that good. But . . . it's still pretending to be someone else. You *could* show them the real you. You could show them the Jelly I see, who I happen to think is freaking *awesome*. I think you might be surprised at how people react. Anyway. Think about it, okay?"

He leaves, and I can't move. I'm sitting on my bed, staring at the carpet and hearing his words in my head over and over. *Smart . . . clever . . . you have a real talent for writing . . . you* feel *things . . . freaking* awesome. . . .

No one has ever said anything like that to me before. Ever.

But the idea of performing my song to the whole school and their parents . . . no way.

No. Freaking. Way.

Chapter 26

The next day is Friday. "You OK?" asks Kayma at break. "You've been really quiet all morning. Mr. Lenck hasn't had to tell you off once!"

I open my mouth to do an impression of Mr. Lenck trying to work out what's going on, and then I close it again. Instead, I say, "I don't know. I feel a bit weird, you know?"

"What kind of weird?" asks Kayma.

I shrug. "Sort of . . . mixed-up weird."

"Like a tummy ache?" asks Sanvi. "Do you need to go to the office?" She lowers her voice. "Have you got your . . . *period* again?" Of course, I'd told both of them the next day what had happened. Kayma immediately said, "Yuck!" and Sanvi said, "Wow, you're grown-up now," and I felt quite important, being the first one of us to start.

I shake my head. "It's not that."

"Maybe," says Kayma, a twinkle in her eye, "your body is being taken over by aliens. . . ." She and Sanvi immediately go, "Oh, no!" and do mock terror, their hands over their mouths.

It's no good. They're not used to me being serious. I don't feel brave enough to tell them what Lennon said—because if I did I'd have to tell them about my poems, and then they'd want to read them, and I . . . can't. They're so used to me being the clown. So that's what I give them.

"Oh my gosh, you're right!" I exclaim, clapping my hands to my stomach. "I think . . . I think it's going to . . . *aaargh*!" I fall to the ground, writhing, spasming, gargling, miming an alien bursting out of my stomach. Kayma and Sanvi giggle, and before many seconds have passed a little crowd has gathered, watching me. I die heroically, gasping out, "Tell my mother . . . the money is in the . . . aarrgghhh . . ."

The spectators drift away. I hear someone saying,

"Doesn't she know when to stop?" and suddenly my performance doesn't feel quite so much fun after all. The enjoyment I got from knowing people were watching fizzles out, like air from a punctured balloon.

The weird feeling returns, like something inside me is really trying to get out but can't find the way. What if people don't find me funny anymore? What will I do then?

When to stop?
When the lights dim?
When the curtain falls?
When the laughter fades?

Then to stop?

But what happens
After the performance
In the darkness?

Mom is behaving strangely during the weekend. She can't seem to settle on anything, keeps picking things up and putting them down again, moving stuff around and then back again. She even opens a bag of chips (unheard of!) and chomps down four before saying, "What on earth am I doing? Here, Jelly, you have the rest. . . ." She passes the bag to me and then, as it leaves her fingers, her gaze suddenly flicks to my stomach, startled, as though she's just remembered that I don't fit into pants anymore, and her hand stays outstretched for a moment, as though she's not sure whether she should snatch back the open bag.

It takes less than a second, I suppose, though the moment feels burned into my memory, especially as it ends with her giving a faint shrug and turning away.

I eat the chips, even though I guess I shouldn't.

On Sunday morning, the phone rings. It's Nan and Grandpa, inviting themselves to dinner again on Wednesday, since they'll "be in the area." Mom's face tightens as she speaks to them, her voice light and airy but her eyes hard. She puts down the phone and goes to make herself another green tea, her third of the day. The phone rings again. "Can you get it?" she calls to me.

I pick up. "Hello?"

"Jelly!" comes Auntie Maggi's voice, bright and very loud. I wince and hold the phone away from my ear. "How *are* you, dahling? It's simply *years* since I've seen you. When are you going to come visit?"

"Um . . ." I say, but it doesn't really matter because Auntie Maggi is steaming ahead at 100 miles per hour.

"I was just saying to your mom the other day, you must be getting so big! Is it ten you are now?"

"Eleven."

"Eleven, no way! Did I miss your birthday? I *didn't*, did I? I'm so terrible at remembering things, you'd think I'd be better at it by now. I've bought a new organizer and I'm determined to write *absolutely everything* in it so I don't forget important things like birthdays and holidays and stuff. So tell me everything! How's school, do you have lots of friends, what do you do for fun, what should I cook you when you come visit?" She pauses, out of breath.

I feel out of breath myself. Auntie Maggi isn't usually like this on the phone. It's as if she's been sped up, like someone pressed "fast-forward" on her remote control. "Er," I say, not sure which question to answer first, but again she doesn't give me time to. Her voice streams on, like chattering sparrows in a hedge, the sounds rising and falling over themselves.

To my enormous relief, Mom comes back from the kitchen with her tea and I hand her the phone.

There's a weird feeling inside me, like I want to do something but I don't know what. I'm all jittery, itchy on the inside of my skin. And at the back of my mind, tapping on an imaginary door, is this little voice saying quietly: You know the talent show . . . ?

No. Don't even think it.

You *could* do your song. . . .

No, no, no, no!

By the time Lennon comes later that day I'm desperate for some sane company. Mom was already twitchy and weird, and since Maggi's phone call she's doubly so. Both of us are like grasshoppers in a jar.

I give Lennon a big hug when he comes in, and he looks surprised but pleased. "Can we play something?" I ask. "I've been practicing."

"Course," he says, removing his guitar. "Let me just say hello to your mom first."

"Careful," I warn. "She's in a funny mood."

"OK." He nods.

I go into the living room and fidget while their voices talk softly in the kitchen. Well, Lennon's voice is soft. Mom's sounds . . . odd, still. Eventually they come out, Lennon leading Mom by the hand. He raises his eyebrows at me but otherwise makes no comment.

Lennon and I play the one about the long and winding road that he played that first time. And then we play my song too, and this time I join in on the singing as well as the harmonica line. Lennon drops his voice so he's only singing quietly, which unnerves me a bit, but he smiles at me reassuringly, and after all it's only him and Mom here, isn't it? So I sing more confidently and at the end he says, "That was *amazing*," and suddenly all the horrid itchy-on-the-inside feelings go away and instead I feel like I've just been dunked in warm honey.

Mom is sipping her tea quietly and not saying anything.

"What did you think, Mom?" I turn to her.

"Oh." She smiles but it looks like an effort. "It was beautiful. Well done, love."

She doesn't sound all that enthusiastic. Why can't she say it was amazing, like Lennon?

"Jelly," Lennon says, "could you do something for me?"

"What?"

He fiddles with the tuning pegs on his guitar. "I . . . I've written your mom a song. I wondered—"

"You've what?" asks Mom, as though suddenly connecting with what's going on.

He looks at her. "I've written you a song. I'd like to sing it to you, but—" He looks at me. "Jelly, would you mind going to your room while I do? I'll gladly play it to you afterward, but I think your mom should be the first to hear it. Would that be OK?"

"Oh! Uh—yeah, of course." I get up, feeling suddenly flustered. *Is he going to propose to my mom in song?* That would be so romantic! I rush out, trying to keep the biggest smile off my face, and go to my room. Of course, I don't *stay* there—that would be stupid! No—instead I come straight out again and tiptoe back along the hall. No way am I missing this moment!

"Lennon," I hear Mom say. I press myself against the hallway wall so they can't see me. "Look, I need to talk to you—"

"Will you let me sing this first?" Lennon says, and his voice sounds soft. "Please, Arlene. I really want you to hear it."

There's a small pause, and then my mom makes a little sighing noise and says, "All right."

Lennon starts to play. And then he starts to sing. It's a song about a boy who fell in love with a girl and she broke his heart. The boy was so hurt, so lost, that he resolved to keep his heart locked up so that it couldn't be broken again. And then, years after his lost love, he met another girl, one with eyes of fire and water and air, and a heart that needed caring for, because this girl was also lost and broken in her own way. The boy tells himself he mustn't fall again, but he can't help himself, and now he can't imagine life without the girl, and the chorus repeats over and over . . .

Can't you see? This is me
Where you are is where I want to be
When I'm with you, it all seems new
The past can heal with love that's true
You make me bigger, make me stronger
Make me better, make me long for
You
Only you

I stand and lean against the wall and tears stream down my face because this is what Lennon was saying to me the other day: that music and poetry can let other people see into your soul and your heart. Singing your own words shows everyone who you really are, your hopes and dreams and cares and fears. You're risking everything by singing it—but if you don't, those words and thoughts and feelings stay locked up inside you, as you pretend to be someone else.

I think, as I listen, that Lennon is very, very brave to sing such things to my mother.

And if he can do it, then so can I.

Chapter 27

It's some time before Lennon comes to find me. By then, of course, I'm safely back in my bedroom, having opened and closed the door very, very quietly. I look up. "Everything OK?"

"Yeah." He smiles, though I can't help feeling there's something slightly unsure about it. "I think she's a bit surprised. She said no one's ever done anything like that for her before."

I cast my mind back over Mom's previous boyfriends. "No," I agree with certainty. "No one's *ever* done that before. In fact, most of them haven't been very nice to her at all."

"I can't understand that," he says. "Your mom is one of the kindest, sweetest, most beautiful souls I've ever met."

I open my mouth to agree that of course she's beautiful, and then realize what he said. He didn't say she was beautiful, he said she had a beautiful *soul*.

I'm not sure I know what a soul is really. I think it must be somewhere in your tummy. We once had a visit from a member of the priesthood. He talked about the soul being a person's essence—something that could go on after death. He didn't mention it being beautiful though. I imagined it was a kind of blob. But when Lennon says Mom has a beautiful soul, it makes it sound like something swirly and sparkly, like glitter on the breeze.

"Jelly?"

I realize I've just been frowning in a puzzled way at him. "Sorry, what?" I say.

He smiles. "We're going to order in pizza and watch something. Want to come join us?"

"Yes," I say. He turns to go. "Wait though. I wanted to say: I'm going to do my song in The K Factor. Um . . . if you'll come too, I mean. And help me."

The biggest smile I've ever seen spreads across his face. But he simply says, "Cool. That's cool. Of course I'll be there."

Opening

What is a bud if it doesn't bloom?
What is the point of a locked-up room?
What is a book that's never read?
What is a dough that's never bread?
Why have words if not to speak?
Why be the same and not unique?
Why have wings if not to fly?
Why give up instead of try?
When will "soon" become "today"?
When will fears be put away?
When will I let people see
Beyond the battlements to me?

Chapter 28

I wake up the next morning feeling different. The thought of singing my song in The K Factor still scares me silly, but knowing it's the right thing to do brings a kind of calmness. Well, more like terrified acceptance. It's Monday, so I'll need to go to see Mrs. Belize today to explain that I want to change my act.

I hope she doesn't make a fuss about it. I don't know if anyone has changed their act before. I'd like to keep it a secret, so that no one knows until the actual night. That way, I tell myself, I can still back out if I need to.

But I won't back out. I *want* to sing my song, I want to let everyone see that I'm more than jokes and a size.

I get up with enthusiasm and put on my school clothes. The apartment is quiet, but maybe Mom is sleeping in a bit. It doesn't matter—I can get my own breakfast.

I sit at the table eating my cereal when I become aware of a faint noise from Mom's room.

The hairs prickle on the back of my neck as a cold chill creeps through me. No, no . . . it can't be. . . .

I push open her door very gently. She is there, huddled under the duvet.

Crying.

There is no sign of Lennon, but I'm *sure* he was staying over last night.

"Mom," I say gently, sitting on the bed next to her. "Mom, what is it?"

Slowly she turns over. Her face is streaked with tears and her eyes are all swollen and red. "Oh, hi, darling. Sorry. I didn't want you to hear me."

"Mom, what's happened? Where's Lennon?"

She sits up and blows her nose. Then she sighs and says, in a voice as quiet and gray as mist, "He's gone."

"Gone? What do you mean, gone?"

"I mean gone. We're over. Here we go again and all that."

I can't take it in. The cereal clogs in my throat. "What? What—*why*?"

"You wouldn't understand," she says, waving the tissue at me. "You're too young."

"*Mom.* He's the best thing that ever happened to us!"

"Things aren't as simple as that."

I get up off the bed. I'm struggling to understand. "Mom, he wrote you a *song.*"

"Jelly—" her voice sharpens "—I don't want to talk about it."

"But . . ." My confusion is turning to anger. *He wrote me a song too and I was going to sing it and I made a big decision about it and now . . .* "But what about *me*? He's my friend too!"

"Well, I'm sorry," she says, turning away from me and curling up again. "It's not about you."

I stare at the lump in the bed, and at that moment I hate my mother. Hate her with a blind fury, a bitter passion. Because she's ruined everything. Taken away the only person I could really talk to.

And she has *no idea* what that means to me.

I turn away, pick up my school bag, and leave the apartment without saying another word. I'm half an hour early so I sit in the park and glower at the gravel.

Some people feel better after being on their own for a bit. Not me. It just makes things worse. Stuff goes around and around in my head: meeting Lennon in the coffee shop before I knew who he was, Mom's eyes shining softly, him lending me his harmonica, showing him my poetry . . .

He made me feel better about myself. He made Mom feel good, I know he did! So what happened?

I end up being late to school because I lose track of time in the park. I have to sign in at the office and, because my luck is bad, Mrs. Belize is in the office when I arrive. "Angelica," she says, giving me a penetrating glance, "everything all right? Why are you late?"

I open my mouth to say, "Sorry, miss," but instead what comes out is, "Oh, Mrs. Belize, you wouldn't *believe* what happened on my way to school this morning. There was this little old man crossing the road, right, and he was walking like this—" I do a demonstration of an elderly man shuffling extremely slowly "—and I went over to help him, and he went completely mental at me! Seems he thought I was a spy from the Cold War, and he broke into this massive rant!" (Here I adopt what could possibly be a French or Russian accent that occasionally slips into Welsh.) "*Leetle gurrl, ha! You arrre a spy, I tell you, and—*'"

"That's enough," says Mrs. Belize crisply, and I shut my mouth abruptly. The words just poured out of me, I didn't have any control. Miss Rasheed, the receptionist, is hiding a grin behind her hand, but Mrs. Belize is not in the tiniest bit amused. "I'm not in the mood, Angelica. I've been hearing reports about you from Mr. Lenck, and I'm not impressed with your lack of concentration and your constant habit of playing the fool. And don't use the word 'mental' in that context, it's insulting and unacceptable."

My face burns. "Sorry, Mrs. Belize."

She opens the door to let me through. "I'm keeping an eye on you, young lady."

Something inside me is fizzing, like when you open a bottle of soda. I can't work out if it's shame or rebellion or . . . I don't even think I have the right kinds of words for it. It makes me feel very . . . *alive*. Like everything is brighter and louder and faster. I stride down the corridor and can barely feel my feet touching the ground.

"Helloooo!" I call out as I step into the doorway of the classroom and strike a pose. "Did y'all miss me?"

Mr. Lenck frowns. "Angelica, you're late. Class has already started. Please sit down quietly." I roll my eyes as I make my way to my seat, but although a couple of people laugh, most of them don't. My breath speeds up. I don't like it when people don't laugh. I'll have to try harder.

Over the course of the morning I impersonate each of the staff one at a time. Ms. Jones takes the spelling test, not me. Mr. Harding hands out the paints and brushes in art. And Miss Rasheed, all fluttery nerves, isn't sure whether she's doing her math questions right or not. My friends catch on quite quickly. Kayma giggles, but Sanvi says anxiously, "Be careful, Jelly. You'll get in trouble."

It takes Mr. Lenck a while to catch on, and by then I'm impatient with not getting the responses I need. So I ramp it up, and soon Mr. Lenck finds he's trying to teach himself. "The square root of forty-nine," he says, writing on the board, "is seven, and so the final answer must be four. Everyone get it?"

I put up my hand. "Yes, Angelica?"

"Mr. Lenck," I say, in his voice, "I don't know what you think you're doing, but the answer can't possibly be four." I sniff. "It's obviously three." I grin at him.

There is a long pause, and the room is suddenly,

horribly silent. Mr. Lenck looks at me: a blank, tired look.

And I know, with absolute certainty, that this time I have gone too far.

Without saying a word, he sits down at his desk and reaches for a yellow slip of paper and a pen. As he writes, I can feel the eyes of everyone else in the room. Sanvi reaches for my hand under the table, but I snatch it away.

Mr. Lenck finishes, stands up, and holds out the piece of paper to me. "Take this to Mrs. Belize's office. Now."

I push back my chair, and one of the legs tangles on a bag on the floor. I shove it with more strength than it needs, and the chair falls over. Someone snickers. In that split second I decide to leave the chair where it is. I take the paper from Mr. Lenck without looking at him and walk straight out of the room.

As soon as I'm in the corridor, I start to shake. My whole body quivers, my legs go weak, and I have to put a hand on the wall to steady myself. I don't read what he's written on the paper, even though he hasn't folded it. I don't need to. I know what kind of trouble I'm in.

No one is ever sent to Mrs. Belize, apart from Harry, who has anger issues.

It's not pleasant. Mrs. Belize takes one look at the

paper and her face darkens in disappointment and annoyance. Her lips press together. "Sit down," she says.

I sit on the chair opposite her desk and stare at a weird metal frame in front of me, with silver balls hanging on thin threads. If you lift the ball at one end and let go, it slams into the one next to it, and the ball at the other end suddenly springs out in reaction. Then that ball swings back, and the first ball jumps out, and it goes on and on. The balls in the middle stay exactly where they are. It feels like a metaphor for something.

"Angelica," says Mrs. Belize, "this behavior needs to stop. Being funny is fine, but not when it repeatedly disrupts lessons. Mr. Lenck has had enough, and frankly I can't blame him."

I keep staring at the metal balls.

"I know you like to be in the spotlight," Mrs. Belize continues, "but there's a fine line between being funny and being disruptive, and you've crossed it. So from now on, it stops. No more impressions of teachers. No more back talk. It's not funny and it's not clever. Most of all, it's not respectful—which, as you know, is one of our core values."

I nod miserably.

"And of course," Mrs. Belize says, with a sigh, "that

means—I'm afraid—no participation in The K Factor final on Friday."

My jaw drops and my eyes open wide. I stare at her. "What?"

She raises her eyebrows at me. "You heard me. You're disqualified from taking part. That will show you just how seriously I'm taking this."

Comedy clown

Idiot fool

Pushing too far

Breaking the rules

Just couldn't stop

Put on the brakes ♪

Hurtling on ♪ ♪ ♪

Until it's <u>too</u> <u>late</u>

Chapter 29

I don't know how I feel. Kayma and Sanvi burst into tears on hearing the news and hug me lots, but I can't cry. I feel sort of . . . numb. Almost like I'm outside my body looking down on myself.

"This is *so* unfair!" Kayma says fiercely, wiping her eyes. "I'm going to go and see Mrs. Belize and tell her she has to let you be in the final."

We both know she's not going to do that of course. She wouldn't dare. No one would. When Mrs. Belize makes a decision, that's it. She doesn't go back on it, ever.

"You could have *won*," Sanvi sobs. "It's the thing you're best at!"

Yes. Pretending to be funny and bubbly and don't-careish . . . that's what I'm best at. Because I've practiced it all my life.

Lennon didn't think it was what I'm best at. He thought I was talented at writing, at feeling, at expressing things.

I can't think about him. It all hurts too much. So I stay floating outside myself, watching my body go through the rest of the day: mechanically eating lunch, walking around the playground, sitting through afternoon lessons. Sanvi keeps holding my hand. She'd be hurt if I told her it isn't helping, so I don't try to pull it away. Both she and Kayma stay protectively close to me, which means I don't need to pretend to be all right—which is good, because I seem to have lost all my pretending.

When I get home, Mom is working as usual. She comes out to take a cup of tea with me, and I can see by her eyes that she's been crying. She asks me about my day and I answer in short phrases. I don't tell her about Mrs. Belize and being disqualified from The K Factor.

I am ashamed.

I open my poetry book and stare at the blank page.

Nothing comes. There are no words, no sentences to form.

There is nothing, just a big empty hole inside me.

I drift through Tuesday and Wednesday. People look at me oddly. Everyone's heard about my ban from The K Factor. News spreads fast in school. Even the little kids know who I am and what happened. Will says to me in passing, awkwardly, "Sorry about what happened, Jelly. I thought you were going to win this year."

I nod and thank him. At least, I think I do. It's getting hard to concentrate on what's actually happening around me. I suppose I'm doing and saying the right things, because I complete the work and I answer questions in class, and no one tells me off for getting it wrong, so I guess my body is just carrying on. Without my brain—or my soul? Maybe it is my *soul* that is in hiding—or has temporarily moved outside myself.

The trouble is, when you're not sure who you are, it's sort of hard to figure out what's going on.

I thought I knew who I was, but now I don't. And everyone else thinks I'm the same as I always was. Every now and then someone cracks a joke in class, and people look at me expectantly—and I just shrug. I don't think that Jelly is coming back.

Mom is quiet and sad too, so she doesn't notice I'm not myself. Or maybe she thinks it's just because I'm sad about her and Lennon splitting up. On Wednesday when I get home, she's vacuuming the carpet and plumping the cushions, and I remember that Nan and Grandpa are coming over for dinner.

They turn up promptly at five, and Grandpa as usual starts complaining: This time it's other drivers on the road. It's one of his favorite topics. Mom and Nan escape to the kitchen on the pretext of cooking the vegetables, and I sit and stare at the newly cleaned living room carpet while Grandpa drones on. "She was sitting in the outside lane doing bang-on fifty, and I signaled her but she wouldn't move over, and there was *plenty* of room in the inside lane!"

I happen to know that the road Grandpa is referring to has a speed limit of fifty, but I don't bother to point this out. To Grandpa, speed limits are for other people.

"And then when I pulled over so I could pass her on the inside, she moved right in front of me! I nearly crashed into her, the stupid woman." He shakes his head. "Women drivers—they're so dangerous."

I give a deep sigh.

"What's the matter with you today?" he demands, taking another sip of wine. "Cat got your tongue?"

"A cat?" I say slowly. "Why should a cat get my tongue?"

Grandpa snorts. "I don't know, it's just one of those sayings. I meant you're very quiet."

"Well," I say softly, feeling like the words are just coming out by themselves, "you don't give me a chance to say much."

He stares at me and his eyes narrow. "Smart, aren't you? Always fond of the back talk. Got no respect, that's your problem. Like all young people."

"We're not all the same," I say dreamily. "All young people—that's not really a thing. It's like saying all old people. Or all white people. Or all middle-aged men with opinions." A slight smile tugs at the corners of my mouth. I am aware of a faint tingling in the air around me. Tiny sparks of something dangerous.

There is a pause, and then Grandpa shouts to the kitchen, making me jump. "Arlene! What's got into this child of yours today? Is she ill?"

Mom comes in, clutching a small knife and a potato. "Pardon? What do you mean?"

Grandpa jerks a thumb toward me. "Talking nonsense. Like something's wrong with her brain."

"What are you talking about?" Mom takes a few steps toward me, puzzled.

I look up and smile at her. "It's all right," I say mildly. "I was just pointing out to Grandpa that he gets things wrong sometimes."

Grandpa's face is slowly turning red. The pinpoint flashes around me are multiplying, I can see them from my place outside the scene. I know he is getting angry, and I don't care. "This kid of yours," he snarls, "should learn some respect. I've always said so, haven't I, Hilary?"

Nan, who has been hovering in the doorway like a shadow, shrinks back.

"That's the trouble," Grandpa goes on, putting down his wineglass and inching forward on his chair, "with no decent discipline. You've never been strict enough with her, Arlene. Letting her talk to people like that! And all this silly mimicking. It's rude and bad behavior, and if there was a man around the house, he'd soon sort it out! I never let *you* speak to me like that."

"No," murmurs Mom, "you didn't."

I look at Grandpa, clear-eyed. "You don't let anyone

speak to you in the way you speak to them. If you could only hear yourself."

Grandpa stands up. "Apologize, young woman!" he snaps. "Right now." He's pointing at the floor, almost as though he expects me to get down on my knees. "I'm waiting."

"Jelly . . ." breathes Mom, so quietly I almost don't hear her.

The tingling pinpricks flow together like lightning in the air around me. And suddenly, like a giant wave, they flood into me, pulsing through my veins, jolting me to my feet, my heart racing and my head clearing until I see only one thing: what is right and what needs to be said.

I plant my feet squarely on the floor. I feel rooted, like energy is flowing from the ground into my body, up out of my head and into the air. "I will not apologize to you," I say to Grandpa, and it is *me* speaking, not some mechanical body. "You have never apologized to *me*. You criticize everything about me: what I like, how I look, what I eat. You say hurtful things so often I think you must *like* it. You like hurting other people. You say hurtful things to Mom and to Nan, and they are afraid of you, so they don't say anything back. But—" I look him straight in his narrow, nasty eyes "—my mom is the best mom anyone could ever have and she has given me everything, and that means that I know you are *wrong* and you are *unkind*, and *I am not afraid of you!*"

Grandpa steps forward, and his hand swings up through the air so fast that I barely see it move, and he brings it down, right across the side of my head—or where my head would be if Mom's arm wasn't there, quicker than sight, blocking it. She yelps with the pain of the blow, but then she is standing in front of me, in between me and Grandpa, and she is pale and quivering and I don't think I've ever seen her look like this. It's as though she is filled with cold fire.

"Do not touch my daughter," she says to Grandpa, and her voice is hard like ice and stone and diamond. "You will not hit my child. Not today, not *ever.*"

"She needs to be taught a lesson!" Grandpa blusters. "You should be teaching her how to behave! You were always the weak one!"

Mom's voice shakes with fury. "You're right. I should've been more like Maggi. I should've stood up to you a long time ago. But I will not have you crush my daughter the way you've crushed me all my life. If you can't be civil to my family, you can get out."

"Your family." Grandpa laughs sarcastically. "I *am* your family."

A sudden screeching sound rips through the apartment—the smoke alarm.

"The pan!" gasps Nan, and rushes to the kitchen. The sudden noise distracts us all, and Mom runs after Nan, while I grab a cushion and dash to the hallway, flapping the cushion back and forth underneath the alarm to get it to stop.

By the time Nan has doused the burnt saucepan in the sink and Mom has opened the window, and the awful piercing noise has stopped, Grandpa has his coat on and is opening the front door, car keys in hand. "Hilary," he says, and leaves.

Nan looks from me to Mom in dismay. No one says anything. She hugs us both and then leaves too.

The door closes behind them.

Chapter 30

"Well," says Mom, and swallows. "Well."

"Yeah," I say.

The air smells of burnt metal, a tang on my tongue. I look down at my hands. They don't fizz with energy now. Instead there's a quiet kind of hum to them, like the blood is singing under the skin, ebbing and flowing through the veins. I turn my hands over to look at the palms, marveling. I don't quite know what just happened, but it's like I flew back into my body.

There's a strange noise behind me, and I turn to see Mom, her shoulders shaking, face white, cheeks wet with tears that stream down in rivers. She leans against the wall so that she doesn't slide to the floor.

"Mom . . ." I say, and go to help her.

We sit on the sofa together and I hold her hands. "You saved me," I say. "He was going to hit me, and you saved me."

"Of course I did," she says. "I won't let anyone hurt you. You're my baby."

"Are you OK?" I ask, which seems like a silly question but I don't know how else to put it.

She gives me a watery smile. "Oh, I dunno. Yes, no, maybe. It's all been a bit of a shock. I've never stood up to Grandpa before. No one apart from Maggi has. And then you . . ." She strokes my hair. "You were amazing. So strong and calm and wise, and true. Everything you said was true." She pauses a moment and then says, "I wish I could be more like you."

My mouth falls open. "More like *me*?" I stammer. "Why?"

"You're so . . . sorted," Mom says. "You just go through life, brushing things aside. You don't let things get to you. You stand up for yourself."

I stare at her, stunned. She doesn't know. But then,

how could she? I've fooled her, just like I've fooled everyone else, all this time.

Sometimes you know you're in an important moment. Balancing on a tightrope of choices.

Option One, Option Two . . . who knows how many there are? Pick the wrong one, and you slip and fall and you'll never get back up on that tightrope again. Pick the right one . . . take a step . . . another step . . . and you might make it to your destination.

"I have to show you something," I say to Mom.

I get up and go to my room and fetch the book. I sit next to her again, and I lay the book in her lap.

"What's this?" she says, and opens it.

She turns the pages, reading and breathing, and, beside her, I read and breathe too. Those are my words, my insides, my blood and tears on those pages, through squiggles that shouldn't convey anything because they're just lines and curves, but somehow . . .

"Oh, Jelly," she whispers, "these are . . . wow. I never knew you felt like this. Some of these are so . . . angry. Painful. Why didn't you tell me?"

"It was easier not to," I say simply.

She stops at the poem about love and music being like honey and ice, and after a moment she gives a sniff and wipes at her face. "Yes," she says. "It's just like that. You clever thing."

I turn the pages until I find the poem that Lennon set to music. She reads it and looks at me, baffled. "This is Lennon's song."

"No," I say, "it's *my* song. He set my poem to music. I was going to sing it in The K Factor and he was going to accompany me on guitar."

Her face crumples. "Oh," she says. "Oh, darling, I'm so sorry. I've ruined everything, haven't I?"

I put my arms around her. "Does it have to be ruined?" I whisper. "Can't you fix it?"

She sighs deeply and pulls back. "He won't want me, Jelly. They never do, in the end."

"But he loved you," I say. "What went wrong?"

"Nothing," she says with a half laugh. "He's perfect. Kind, thoughtful, talented, gorgeous, sweet . . ."

"I don't understand," I say. "I thought that's what you wanted."

"He's too good for me," Mom says. "Oh, Jelly, why would he want me? I'm nothing special. It's better for me to get out before things go wrong."

"Nothing special?" I exclaim. "*Nothing special?!* You're *everything* special! You're kind and thoughtful and hardworking, and you're brave and beautiful—"

She laughs. "You're my daughter—you're bound to say stuff like that. But at some point I always do something wrong, and then they get tired of me . . . and then they leave. They all leave."

"Lennon isn't like the others," I say firmly.

"No," she agrees, "he's better. Much better. That's why I don't want to ruin it."

You know when someone says something that just makes you go "AAARGH!" on the inside, but you can't say it because then they'd be upset? I want to shout, "But you've *already* ruined it!" but of course that wouldn't be kind or helpful, so I press my lips together and think very, very hard about what to say next.

"Mom," I say, and I choose my exact words oh-so-very-carefully, "do you know what Lennon told me? He said you were a beautiful soul. He didn't say you were pretty or skinny or any of that. He said you were beautiful *on the inside*. He doesn't see what everyone else sees. He saw you, and he saw *me*—the real me—the one I've been hiding. Lennon made me feel stronger and better, like I could be more than the funny one. And he made you laugh. Really laugh, I mean, not fake-laughing like you used to do with Chris."

She looks startled. "I did?"

"Yes. Lennon makes us . . . *real*, Mom. He makes us real."

She looks down at her hands and breathes out a long breath. "Have I been very stupid?"

"Yes," I say. "Very. Dumb, in fact. Really obtuse."

She snorts a laugh and looks at me. "I love you, Angelica."

"I love you too, Mom. Text him."

"Oh, I can't."

"Do it."

"I don't know what to say."

"Tell him you made a mistake and you're sorry." As I say it, I think of Kayma and Sanvi. I should have trusted them with how I was feeling too. I should have let them in. They're my friends, they would be there for me. Tomorrow I'll tell them everything: all about my poetry and my secret fears.

Mom reaches for her phone and types with shaking hands. The text sends and we wait expectantly.

Nothing happens.

The phone stays silent.

Mom laughs shakily. "How long are we going to sit here?"

My stomach suddenly rumbles. "Did we miss dinner?" I say in alarm.

"We did!" Mom leaps up. "The meat's still in the oven! Oh, it'll be completely overcooked by now. I'll have to throw it out."

We eat SpaghettiOs on toast and grate cheese over the top and wait for Lennon to reply.

The phone stays silent.

As the minutes tick past I feel more and more tired. Mom doesn't mention Nan and Grandpa and neither do I. There isn't anything to say about them anyway. Both of us just want to hear from Lennon. But he doesn't call.

I get into my pajamas and wash my face. And then, as I'm brushing my teeth, I hear the sound of a text, and I swallow my toothpaste by accident and rush back to the living room. "What did he say, what did he say?" I gurgle, choking slightly.

Mom nearly deletes the message by accident, her hands are shaking again. "He says . . . he says: 'Thank you. I'll get back to you tomorrow.'" She stares at me.

"That's all?" I'm disappointed. For some reason I thought he would say he forgave her and he was on his way over. . . . For a moment I'd thought that maybe fairy tales were real after all.

"We have to wait," Mom says, and she blinks too many times. "It's only fair really." She smiles brightly at me with wet eyes. "Get some sleep, gorgeous girl. How lucky I am to have you. You're the best thing that ever happened to me."

"Love you, Mom."

"Love you, Jelly."

Chapter 31

There's no further text in the morning, but I am feeling calmer. Yesterday was kind of epic. I almost can't believe it really happened—me standing up to Grandpa, and Mom dashing in to protect me like some white knight on a horse, or whatever the saying is.

It feels like yesterday was a turning point. Like I'd been scattered, bits of my soul and my feelings, all thrown into the air and floating around—and then they were all pulled back into me and they formed a new pattern: a new Jelly.

I'm glad I showed Mom my poetry. Isn't it funny when you suddenly discover that someone else worries about exactly the same things you do? Mom thought she wasn't good enough for Lennon. I've never really felt good enough for . . . for the world, I suppose, because of my size. Both of us were afraid of being seen for who we really are inside. And now . . . now we're not. Or not as much anyway. I set off to school feeling strangely zen-like. (I heard about zen once. It's to do with inner peace and, I think, motorcycles.)

When I see Sanvi in the playground, I go over to her and say, "Sanvi, there's something I should tell you."

She immediately looks worried. "What is it?"

Kayma comes running over, full of annoyance over something Hula did this morning.

"Shh!" Sanvi says, which is *most* unlike her. "Jelly's got something to say."

Kayma turns to me. "What?"

So I tell them both. About how I worry about my weight, how everyone is thinner than me and sometimes that really, really bothers me, how I use humor to distract people from seeing I might be upset, how Mom had the perfect boyfriend who could have joined our family and maybe I could even have had a dad, and how I would really, really like that, but it's gone wrong and I'm sad about it. How I write poems at home that I've never dared show anyone.

The bell goes as they're listening, and Kayma says, "Oh, shoot," and Sanvi says, "Keep talking, Jelly," and she links arms with me as we walk into school.

They don't really have a chance to say much before Mr. Lenck takes attendance and starts the lesson, but Sanvi squeezes my hand really hard, and Kayma gives me a hug as she goes past to collect some paper, and those little things really help. At break time I talk some more, and they listen, and Verity comes past at one point and sees I'm upset and sneers, and Kayma jumps up and challenges her to a fight, which makes me laugh but also strangely proud and grateful.

"Wow," says Sanvi every now and then. "That's . . . wow."

"Can I see your poems?" Kayma asks. "Are any of them funny?"

"Er . . . not really," I admit. "Most of them are kind of sad or angry or confused."

"Oh," she says. "What was the one like that got turned into a song?"

"A bit sad," I say, with a smile. "It's about putting on a happy face even when I don't feel like it."

"I do that sometimes," says Sanvi unexpectedly.

"You do?"

"Well—" she looks from me to Kayma and back again "—we all do it, don't we? It's like when we did that poem about the mask in English. The happy face is the mask." She gives a sad little smile. "My parents have been arguing quite a lot recently. It makes me afraid that . . . I don't know. Maybe I should try writing a poem about it."

I give her a hug. "Maybe you should. I'm sorry—that sounds horrible."

"I'm jealous of Hula," Kayma confesses suddenly. "You know when I said I always say what I really feel? It's not exactly true. She gets all the special treatment because everyone feels guilty about her arm, so she's always the one to get the extra treat and that kind of thing. Sometimes I wish I'd been in the accident too so that people would make me special." She goes red. "I know it's really wrong to wish that. I feel bad about it."

Sanvi and I hug her too. "Sounds like your poem could be really angry," I suggest.

Kayma laughs. "Yeah—it *so* could."

Sanvi says, "You should tell Mrs. Belize all of this. I bet she'd let you back in The K Factor if she knew what was behind everything."

I shrug. "It's OK. I don't want to do my impressions

anyway. And I can't do the song without Lennon. Besides, the final is tomorrow night. There wouldn't be time to practice or anything."

The other two nod. "I probably won't go either then," says Kayma. "I was only coming to cheer you on."

Sanvi takes my arm. "We could do something else instead," she says. "Who needs a talent show? We've got friends."

It's the cheesiest line ever, but I'm glad she said it.

That afternoon, I burst through the door to our apartment. "Mom! Mom, has he called back?"

She comes out of her room, on the phone and giving me that "don't make a loud noise" look. "Yup, that's fine," she says into the phone. "As long as next Tuesday is OK. I'm really sorry I can't get it to you before then, it's out of my hands . . . Yep . . . Yep, OK. All right then . . . Yes, the minute it comes in . . . All right. Talk soon, bye!" She hangs up. "Hello, you."

I give her a big hug. "Has he texted you?"

"No."

I draw back. "What? Not at all?"

"No. I sent him another, just saying . . . oh, saying

nothing really. But he hasn't . . . he hasn't texted." She does that expression when people are trying to be brave. "I think maybe we just need to accept it. . . . He's not coming back."

"Oh." I sink into a chair at the table. "Oh. Well, that's . . . that's . . ."

"Yeah. I know. Cup of tea?"

"Yeah, all right." It's eighty degrees today, but still we have tea. That's what you do, isn't it?

Her phone beeps as she goes to the kitchen and she sighs. "That'll be Maggi again. She's had your nan on the phone, all upset about yesterday. I don't really—" She breaks off, and I hear a gasp.

"What?" I call.

"It's him."

I leap up. "Lennon?"

"Yes. He—oh. Well, is that good or bad? I don't know. Jelly, what's this about?" She holds out the phone so I can read the message:

King's Arms, 7pm. Bring Jelly.

I stare at it. Adults are so confusing. Why can't they say what they mean? But then I guess maybe I haven't been great at doing that either. Humans, right? We do *so* like to make things complicated.

We go, of course. Mom is a blubbering wreck, dropping her keys, and forgetting her purse, and catching her floaty scarf in the door as we leave and having to go back in and change it for an almost identical one and . . .

I'm really glad it's not me who's in love with Lennon, if this is what love does to people. My mom has been replaced by a complete idiot. I have to keep saying, "Come on, Mom, you can do this." She grabs my hand and holds it very tightly.

It's a Thursday evening in late spring and it's warm, so lots of people have decided to go to the King's Arms and stand around outside, holding their drinks and blocking the doorway. I feel young and uncomfortable. Why did Lennon tell Mom to bring me? Wouldn't it have been better to meet her alone?

Then I hear music, and I know why.

Lennon's band is playing. Mom's hand grips mine as we push our way through the throng of people.

There are only three of them in this band: Lennon singing and playing guitar, a woman playing a double bass, and a man on a drum kit. It's probably just as well there aren't more, as they're squashed into quite a small space. The room is stifling.

The song finishes just as we get near enough to see, and a smattering of applause breaks out. "Thanks," says Lennon. Then he sees us. Well, to be fair, he sees Mom. I mean, I guess he knows I'm there too, but he doesn't look at me. He clears his throat. "This next song . . . it's new. In fact, this'll be its first tryout. Hopefully we're up to speed on it." He grins at the bass player and the drummer. "It's a last-minute addition to our set, but I wanted to include it because it's for someone very special who's here this evening."

A whole bunch of eyes swivel in our direction, which is really unnerving. Mom goes bright red and squeezes my hand so tightly I wince.

The song starts, and even though it's a hot evening, even though people have come here to have a drink and a chat, silence falls over the audience. It's the sort of song that pulls you in and makes you *feel*. Everyone watches and listens, even the big burly guys closest to the bar who have vests and tattoos.

Lennon's voice is strong and he sings with such feeling I'm almost embarrassed. It's one thing to hear it in the privacy of our living room, quite another in a public place crowded with strangers.

> *You make me bigger, make me stronger*
> *Make me better, make me long for*
> *You*
> *Only you*

When the song dies away there's a huge cheer, which makes me jump in shock. Lennon nods and thanks people, and then he says, "Guys, we're going to take a short break, OK? Back in five." He takes off his guitar and threads his way through the crowd to us. I know loads of people are stealing glances, even though they're pretending to talk to one another again.

Lennon stands in front of my mom and says, "Hi, Arlene. Hi, Jelly."

"Hi," I say automatically.

"Did you want to talk?" he says to Mom.

"Not really," she says, and I want to scream in frustration. She's doing it *again*!

But—no, she isn't. Instead she's kissing Lennon, right there, in the middle of the pub, in front of everyone.

Oh my *gosh*, this is so embarrassing.

I don't know where to look, so I stare at the floor and then the door, and then at some people, but they're cheering at the sight, so that's no good. I mean, I'm pleased, obviously, because it means they're getting back together again, but honestly I'd rather this wasn't happening here, right now, with an audience.

I'm just wondering whether I should go and stand outside and wait until it's over, when suddenly it is over, and Lennon is holding out a hand to me and smiling. "Hey, Jelly," he says, "see what happens when you bare your soul to everyone onstage?"

"I'm good with the cheering," I say airily, "but if anyone tries to kiss me, I'll kick their butt."

He laughs. "Fair enough. I have to say, it's the first time it's ever happened to me." He looks down at Mom's shining face. "Though I hope not the last."

"Oh, yuck," I say. "Please don't or I might be sick."

"Sorry." He's laughing again. "How are you? I'm so glad you both came. Now I can accompany you in the talent show tomorrow, like we planned." Then he sees my face fall. "What's happened?"

Chapter 32

On Friday morning Lennon and Mom come to school with me. While I head to my class, they ask if they can see Mrs. Belize.

I can't concentrate on anything Mr. Lenck says. He might as well be speaking Swahili. When Miss Rasheed appears in the doorway, my heart leaps. "Sorry to interrupt," she says. "Could Mrs. Belize borrow Angelica for a moment?"

Mr. Lenck looks puzzled. "Sure," he says.

I know everyone is staring at me as I walk to the doorway. I know they're wondering why I've been called to the principal's office. My heart is thumping a samba as

I follow Miss Rasheed. Has it worked? Has she changed her mind?

My palms are sweaty and I wipe them on my skirt. Mrs. Belize is sitting behind her desk, and Mom and Lennon are sitting opposite. Lennon gives me a wink as I come in and my breath catches. Does that mean . . . ?

"Have a seat, Angelica," says Mrs. Belize, indicating a chair next to Mom. I sit down. I should blink. I think I've forgotten how.

"Now," says Mrs. Belize, "I've been having a very useful discussion with your mom and Mr. Maloney here."

Maloney? His surname is Maloney? How come I didn't know this?! *Lennon Maloney.* It sounds cool.

"And I gather things have been quite tricky for you at home recently," Mrs. Belize continues. "I'm sorry you didn't feel able to talk to anyone here at school about it, but I understand that sometimes that can be difficult, to open up to people."

It's nice that she's being all sympathetic and everything, but I just want to shout, "CAN I BE IN THE K FACTOR AFTER ALL??" I dig my teeth into my lower lip to stop myself saying anything because I *know* what happens when I open my mouth without thinking first.

"I would like to put a support plan in place for you,

Angelica," Mrs. Belize says, and if my eyes were lasers they'd have burned a hole right through her by now, I'm staring *that* hard. "I'd like you to see Mrs. Coulson once a week, our guidance counselor, just to keep abreast with your situation."

She said "breast." I think I might explode with hysteria.

"But in the short term it appears there is something the school can do to support you in a rather . . . unusual way." Mrs. Belize pauses. "I gather you and Mr. Maloney here have written a song. Not a comedic song, a serious one, based on a poem you wrote. I have to say, I'm very excited by this idea, and also that you have apparently written a lot of poetry. It's a side of you we haven't seen here at Kingswood, but I think it's a wonderful step that you feel able to share it now. I shall write to the head of English at Marston Junior High and ask him to look out for you."

I gulp. That's . . . cool . . . I guess. *Get to the point!*

"Anyway, given the circumstances, I think it would be reasonable of the school to offer you a platform to perform this song before the end of term. A kind of celebration of your so-far-hidden talents." She smiles. I have been listening so hard, but I can't work out whether

she's actually said it or not. My confusion must be showing on my face.

"Jelly," says Mom gently, "Mrs. Belize says you can
perform tonight in The K Factor."

Oh! Oh.

Oh, good.

Wow, I must be really happy about that. Aren't I?

"Jelly?" Mom says, and I realize everyone is looking at me.

I let out a very long breath, and then I say, "Cool.
Yeah, I mean, thanks."

They all laugh, and I think that's a good thing, but
my head is buzzing so much I honestly can't tell.

The hall is packed. I don't think I've ever seen so many
people in it. I'm sure it's breaking fire regulations.
Parents and kids are standing at the sides and trying to
take photos, and younger siblings are wailing or running
about, and it's a kind of chaos.

I sit through the whole of the first half, tingling and
frightened out of my mind. Lennon and I only had time
for a hasty couple of run-throughs at home before it was
time to come back to school. I haven't yet played the
harmonica bit without a mistake. I'm in a scratchy skirt,
which I only wore because it made Mom go misty-eyed,

and then she insisted on putting makeup on me, so I'm not quite sure I look like me at all. I kind of feel like I should have refused the makeup, because this song is supposed to be about showing people what I'm really like on the inside, but I *would* like to look nice on the outside while I'm doing it. . . .

Sometimes life is way hard to figure out.

The first half has some really good acts in it. A girl in third grade plays the violin and I swear she's good enough to go on *America's Got Talent*. And a boy in fourth grade does a tap-dance routine that makes everyone cheer, and some of the people in the audience stand up. No one does any decent comedy though. A girl tells some jokes but she's not very good. If I were doing my impressions, I'd be feeling fairly confident about my chances, but this song . . . well, let's just say I don't expect to win.

During the intermission, Kayma and Sanvi and I hang around in the corridor, jittery and biting our nails. "I'm *terrified*," Sanvi whispers, her eyes as big as I've ever seen them.

"*You're* terrified?" I exclaim. "It's not even you onstage!"

"I know!" she says. "I just don't want you to mess up!"

"Oh, thanks very much," I say sarcastically. "I'm *bound* to now."

"Nooo," wails Sanvi. "I didn't mean that!"

Kayma laughs. "Sanvi, chill. Jelly, you're going to be amazeballs."

"You're not going to stop doing impressions though, are you?" Sanvi suddenly says. "I mean, now you're doing songs and poetry, you're not going to be serious *all* the time, are you?"

I grin at her. "Sanvi, are you saying you *like* my impressions?"

"Of course I do!" she exclaims. "You're so talented!"

I give her a big hug. "Don't worry," I tell her. "No way am I giving up the fun stuff."

Kayma joins in the hug and we all start squeezing too hard and then I lose my balance and step back right onto Marshall's foot.

"Ow!" he says. "Watch it, Jelly!"

"Sorry," I say. "Really sorry. I didn't see you."

"It's like being trodden on by an elephant," he grumbles.

I take a breath. "That's not a very nice thing to say. I am not an elephant and I don't like being compared to one, thank you."

He stares at me, gobsmacked. "What?"

"Second half!" someone calls from farther down the corridor, and suddenly I don't want to go back into the hall.

Kayma and Sanvi give me more hugs. They know what I'm going to do, though they haven't heard the song. But no one else even knows I've been allowed back into the final. "You're going to be brilliant," they tell me as we go back in and take our seats.

The hall is filling up again and, toward the back, I can see my mom, and Lennon, holding his guitar and trying to keep it from accidentally hitting anyone. It reminds me of the day I first met him in Coffeetastic, and the memory makes me smile.

I'm not on till the end, but for some reason everything goes incredibly fast, and before I know it—before I'm ready—Ms. Jones is standing on the stage. "Now," she says, "you'll see from your programs that we've finished the acts, but in fact we have a last-minute addition."

A puzzled whisper comes from the kids in the audience.

"Angelica Waters qualified for a place in the final," Ms. Jones continues, "but it wasn't until today that we knew she would be performing. Many of you will know that her qualifying act was impressions—"

The pupils start grinning at one another and turning to look at me.

"—but this evening we're going to see another of Angelica's talents, as she's going to sing a song based on a poem she wrote."

Now everyone is staring at me in confusion. This was a mistake. I should never have agreed to it.

"She will be joined onstage by her friend and musician, Lennon Maloney," Ms. Jones says, consulting her piece of paper. "So I'd like you to give a big round of applause to . . . Angelica Waters!"

Stairs aren't usually that hard, are they? I mean, I go upstairs all the time, not thinking about it. But this evening I look at them very carefully as I place my feet one in front of the other. Imagine falling up the stairs on your way—no, don't imagine it! Oh my goodness, my brain is trying to sabotage my own legs!

"Hey, Jelly," Lennon's voice breaks into my internal mayhem. He's pulled up a chair and is sitting down, tuning his guitar. He adopts a New York accent. "How you doin'?"

Automatically I respond in the same accent. "I'm doin' fine. How *you* doin'?"

Those of the audience who can hear us giggle amiably. The sound is reassuring.

The microphone is too low down for me, so I move it up a bit, my palms slipping on the stand. In my pocket is my harmonica. If that slips out of my hands in the middle of the song, I'm going to look *really* dumb.

"Ready?" asks Lennon, and I nod, because if I stand here any longer without something to do or a joke to crack, I think I'll faint.

He starts to play the introduction, and for a terrifying moment, I can't remember the first line. But then it comes. And so does the rest of the song.

HAPPY FACE

by Angelica Waters / Lennon Maloney

C   Em   C   Em   C

Is this me? Is this you?

Em   D

Is this the best that we can do? Hid-ing be-hind a web of lies,

Em   C

hop-ing you can't see in my eyes 1. Tell a joke, be a clown,
2. Life is cool, life is fun,

Em   D

don't let you see when I am down, keep all my wor-ries deep in-side
that's what I tell eve-ry- one No-thing you say can hurt me, see?

Em   C

Don't let you know I cried cos I'm a hap-py face hid-ing an
That's my i-den-ti-ty, cos I'm a

Em   C   Em

emp-ty space, yes I'm a hap-py face But if

G   Em   C   G

you could see be-yond the smile, would you still be there?

Would you want to be my friend, would you ev-en care? Cos I'm a

hap-py face hid-ing an emp-ty space

And if you could see be-yond the smile, would you still be there?

Would you want to be my friend, would you ev-en care? Cos I'm a

1. hap-py face hid-ing an emp-ty space, Yes I'm a
2. hap-py face hid-ing an emp-ty space, Be-ing a
3. big dis-grace to the whole hum-an race, Keep-ing my

smile in place, Rem-em-ber my hap-py face...

Chapter 33

The last note dies away, and for a moment it's as though everyone is frozen in time. My mom, hands to her mouth, eyes streaming with tears (of pride, I hope), Ms. Jones on the end of the front row, dabbing at her eyes with a tissue. The three judges, one of which is indeed Mrs. Belize's daughter, Julie (from *Glee*), gazing at me as though spellbound—and Mrs. Belize herself, who gives an audible sniff, and the silence is broken.

The wall of noise is extraordinary, making me rock on my feet slightly. Cheering and clapping and whooping, and people stomping their feet, and Kayma and Sanvi jumping up and down and yelling, though I can't hear the words.

I don't know what to do for a moment, it's disorientating. And then Lennon stands up next to me and says in my ear, "Take a bow, Jelly. You deserve it."

So I do, and then he gives a little bow before stepping back to clap me, and then I get off the stage because although I've always loved performing, I'm kind of glad it's over and now I just want . . . well. I guess I just want my mom.

Everyone hugs me or pats me as I make my way down the hall, and all the parents are crying and smiling, and I think, *Wow, they must really have liked it*. And Marshall says, "That was awesome, Jelly, and I'm really sorry about what I said," and it all kind of floats around and through my head in a haze. A few rows back, my mom catches my eye and points to the doors that lead into the corridor.

Then the noise drops and I know Ms. Jones is explaining how there will be a ten-minute interval while the judges make their decision. But I don't hear what she says because I'm out in the corridor and Mom is giving me the biggest hug I think I've ever had in my life, whispering into my ear how proud she is of me and how amazing I am and how from now on she's going to think of this moment whenever she needs courage. . . .

And to be honest it's all a bit overwhelming and I sort of burst into tears. Lennon comes to find us, and Mom holds out a hand to him, and he joins in the hug. "Good work, Jelly," is all he says, but it's enough.

Later they announce the winners, and I come in third, just like last year. I go up onstage to collect a miniature trophy, and the cheering and stomping from the audience makes me want to cry with pride. Kayma and Sanvi are screaming and jumping up and down again, and Mom and Lennon are clapping so hard their hands are a blur.

It was worth it. It was all worth it.

"You should have won," Mom tells me as we emerge into the playground.

I look up at the sky, still light, though one star has appeared. "I did," I say. "I did win."

Mom takes my hand, and Lennon takes the other, and we walk home.

For my friends
Kayma and Sanvi
on our first day at Marston High

Long ago when we first met
we talked about our favorite pets
I told you both of my giraffe
It wasn't true but made you
                        laugh
And from then on I knew I'd be
"The funny one" within our three

I made you laugh, I made you smile
But I kept secrets all the while
And wrote them in my little book
And never would have
                        let you look.

But things have changed and so have I
I'm not afraid you'll see me cry
I'll tell you things I couldn't then
The things I only wrote in pen

There's more to life than Option Two
Which I still like, and so do you
I'll still tell jokes and play the fool
I'll probably mess around at school

But Option Two's not all I've got
In my internal feelings pot
When times are hard and not so fun
From now on I'll take Option One

It's our first day in our new place
We all have fake smiles on our face
That's Option Two, but be aware
That Option One is always there

XXX

Acknowledgments

With grateful thanks to the wonderful team at Piccadilly for making my book beautiful on the inside and the outside and helping it to find readers: Fliss Johnston, Talya Baker, Ruth Logan, Ilaria Tarasconi, Tina Mories, Anneka Sandher, Sara Mulvanny, and Dan Newman.

Thanks also to early readers Claire Hosier, Mandie Preston, and Ben Trevail for invaluable feedback, and to Cathy Cassidy for providing such lovely words for me.

Finally, thanks as ever to my family and friends who carry me when I can't stand alone. And to my two amazing daughters—thanks for the cuddles and the terrible jokes. You're both awesome in so many ways.